Ruby
Parker

Film
Star

Also by Rowan Coleman

Ruby Parker: Soap Star

Ruby Parker

Film Star

ROWAN COLEMAN

HarperCollins *Children's Books*

For my very own superstar, Lily

Thank you to Stella Paskins, Gillie Russell and all the team at HarperCollins Children's Books for their support and enthusiasm.

And extra special thanks to my very own focus group – Polly Harris, Laura Day and Emily Fettes – for their excellent opinions and thoughts, and for the gratis promotional work they did on Ruby Parker's behalf with all of their school friends. I appreciate it very much.

First published in Great Britain by HarperCollins *Children's Books* 2007
HarperCollins *Children's Books* is a division of HarperCollins*Publishers* Ltd,
77-85 Fulham Palace Road, Hammersmith, London W6 8JB

www.harpercollinschildrensbooks.co.uk

1

Text copyright © Rowan Coleman 2006

The author asserts the moral right to be identified
as the author of this work.

ISBN -13: 978 0 00 719039 3
ISBN-10: 0 00 719039 5

Printed and bound in England by
Clays Ltd, St Ives plc

Mixed Sources
Product group from well-managed
forests and other controlled sources
www.fsc.org Cert no. SW-COC-1806
© 1996 Forest Stewardship Council
FSC

29 Windhouse Street
Brighton
Sussex

Dear Ruby,

I wanted to write and thank you for the letter you sent me, and anyway you said for me to let you know how I am doing so I thought I would. When I wrote to you I was feeling really low and getting your letter really made me feel better. I took your letter and showed it to my mum and when she read it she looked sort of surprised and cried. I was worried at first but then she gave me a big hug and it was as if she suddenly realised how much her and Dad splitting up was affecting me too. Things are still hard, and I wish it wasn't happening, but at least they are trying to sort things out in a more friendly way now, and Mum lets me see Dad without getting angry.

I read in Teen Girl Magazine that you have left Kensington Heights. I am sorry you won't be playing Angel any more, she was my favourite character in Kensington Heights, the only one who seemed really real. I am glad that Angel had only gone to America though. Maybe one day you will come back and be in the show again. I know you used to get loads and loads of letters from Kensington Heights fans. I expect the show's fan club will get a lot less mail now. I think it will be nice for you to have a break from writing all of those replies! Maybe you should have your own fan club? I wonder what you will be in next. I will definitely watch it whatever it is.

Thanks again.
Lots of love
Naomi Torrence

Chapter One

"If there's one thing I know about this business we call show business,"
Sylvia Lighthouse told me when it was my turn for her inspirational pre-audition pep talk, "it's that success is never down to good fortune alone – you do realise that, don't you, Ruby?" I nodded. I did know, mainly because I knew exactly what she was going to say next. She had been seeing all of us girls who were about to audition for a part in the Imogene Grant movie, *The Lost Treasure of King Arthur*, individually and in alphabetical order. I was last because poor Selena had chicken pox really badly and hadn't stopped crying since she found out she wouldn't be allowed to audition. (I don't blame her, I would cry too if I discovered I was missing out on such an important audition because of chicken pox, even if at that moment a nice warm bed, a pile of DVDs and a bottle of Lucozade did seem like more fun.) Anyway, it meant that I was last, so Nydia, Anne-Marie, Olivia and Scarlett had already told me what

she was going to say, complete with dramatic pauses and eye rolling.

"Good," Sylvia Lighthouse continued, "because success is perhaps ten per cent luck, maybe even ten per cent talent..." She leaned across her desk and fixed me with her steely glare. "...But do you really know what makes a performer successful?"

"Hard work and lots of it," I answered automatically, before realising that the question was supposed to be rhetorical and I wasn't supposed to answer at all but let her tell me. "I mean, probably..." I added hastily, "I don't know really... um... what do *you* think, Ms Lighthouse?" Sylvia Lighthouse arched an orange pencilled eyebrow at me.

"I do hope you are not *too* confident, Ruby," she said, as she examined me. I shook my head energetically. "Acting in a so-called 'soap opera' and auditioning for a movie are two *entirely* different things. Your experience on *Kensington Heights* means nothing at all here."

"Um oh, right," I said, trying to swallow as my throat tightened in fear. "Well, I know that, Ms Lighthouse, and I'm not too confident, not even a bit." And then I wasn't sure if that was the right thing to say either so I added, "But I'll give it my best shot."

I wanted to tell her that all I could think about was

that very soon I'd be standing in front of award-winning film director Art Dubrovnik about to audition for a part in his next movie, quite a big part, with quite a lot of scenes that would be watched in cinemas all over the world. And that every time I thought about it my heart started thumping, my tummy turned to jelly, my mind went completely blank and I started to come out in stress-related blotches. It was almost exactly the same as the first time I had kissed Danny (only without the blotches luckily). Sylvia Lighthouse drew her lips together and looked at me down her very long nose.

"I hope you don't think you have any advantage over the other girls, Ruby," she told me sternly, "just because you were once a TV star. It's a level playing field out there, you know. And, besides, fame is a very fickle thing. I should know."

"I don't," I told her. "Honestly, I don't, Ms Lighthouse. I'm nervous, I'm really, *really* nervous – look!" I pulled open the collar of my school shirt and showed the bright red marks that were flowering on my skin. She looked at them and wrinkled her nose slightly.

"Well, that's good," she told me a little less harshly. "Fear is good as long as you use it. Don't let it stifle you, Ruby. Just remember that this is your moment. This is your chance to be the best that you possibly can be."

She stood up as she finished speaking, flourishing her hands and gazing over the top of my head as if she had just performed the last lines of a play.

I blinked at her. That part hadn't been in everybody else's pep talk.

"I will, Ms Lighthouse," I told her steadily. "I promise."

She smiled at me then, which looked almost as much like a scar as when she frowned.

"Jolly good," she said. "Well off you go then! You don't want to be late!"

When I walked down the front steps of the academy everybody else was already in the minibus. I looked at their faces peering out of the windows and I knew that I had exactly the same expression on my face – as if we were about to be driven to our certain doom, and not to take the chance of a lifetime.

"Remember," my mum had said that morning, "if you don't get it, it's not the end of the world. You're still only a little girl after all."

"I know," I said, letting the whole "little girl" thing go, because secretly she was just as nervous as me. But it was still hard not to think of it as the potential end of the world.

What would the world be like if I didn't get the part? Almost exactly the same as it had been before, which was not too bad a world – a world with a mum and a dad that were at least talking to each other and getting on quite well since Dad moved out. A world with good friends and a very nice, funny boyfriend. A world with a big fat cat, dancing and singing lessons in the morning and acting class right after maths. An ideal world for a lot of people.

But it would still be a different world in one important respect. If I didn't get this part, it would be the first time I had ever failed. Nobody outside the academy had ever really tested my talent before, not even when I was on *Kensington Heights*. I'd never done another real audition, and I had never expected my first one to be quite so big. So although I did know that it wasn't the end of the world if I didn't get the part, it certainly didn't feel that way.

"All set, girls?" Miss Greenstreet called out, as I climbed on to the bus and slid into the seat next to Nydia. She picked up my hand and squeezed it.

"Yes," we all chorused weakly, glancing at each other anxiously.

"Excellent," Miss Greenstreet said. "Off we go, driver!"

None of us really knew what to expect when it came to movie auditions, me least of all. After all, I had only ever auditioned for *Kensington Heights* when I was six. At the time I thought I was just playing dressing-up, so I didn't exactly feel any pressure. And I had been in *Kensington Heights* playing the part of Angel MacFarley, the world's most average girl, ever since, until last summer. It was then that I decided to leave, because I realised that playing Angel wasn't really acting, it was just being me in front of a TV camera. I wanted to stretch myself, to experience new challenges and take new chances.

Except that morning on the bus I wasn't quite sure about any of that. Challenges and chances and all that stuff didn't seem half so appealing just then. In fact, just then, a career as a librarian seemed much more my sort of thing, as really, out of all the girls on the bus, I was the least experienced in auditions.

Anne-Marie had done quite a few commercials, and just recently Nydia landed her first TV part in *Casualty* as "girl with food poisoning" (She was completely brilliant by the way.), so they both knew more about what might happen than I did.

I thought we might have to stand on a stage in a theatre a bit like when we did audition practice at school, or maybe even go to Mr Dubrovnik's suite in some posh hotel. But we didn't. The minibus stopped on Wardour Street in Soho, and Miss Greenstreet smiled at each of us and patted us one by one on the shoulder as we filed out on to the pavement and then up some dark and narrow stairs to the rehearsal rooms which were above an Italian restaurant.

"I thought it would be more glamorous than *this*," Anne-Marie hissed in my ear as she glanced around her.

"Being an actor isn't about *being* glamorous," Nydia said, repeating one of Ms Lighthouse's favourite phrases, "it's about *creating* it."

"What *does* that mean?" I asked. Nydia and Anne-Marie shrugged simultaneously. Sometimes Sylvia Lighthouse's pearls of wisdom could be, well, rather mysterious to say the least.

At the top of the stairs there was a small waiting room with five orange plastic chairs that were probably older than each one of us who were lined up against the wall. The fluorescent lighting flickered every now and then, and hummed loudly. A lady with wiry orange hair, and with thick black-rimmed glasses perched on top of a long pointy nose, magnifying a pair of scarily pale blue fish-like eyes, was waiting for us. She was wearing a very short tartan kilt and green holey tights, and was armed with a clipboard and a scowl that knitted her thick brows into one.

"Hi, I'm Lisa Wells, assistant director on *The Lost Treasure of King Arthur*," she said briskly in an American accent, leading me to guess that she must be American. "This is how it's going to be. I hope you are all properly prepared and that you know your lines because I'm going to be sending you in one at a time in alphabetical order." I sighed inwardly. That meant I would be the last to go in again. And the one with the longest time to get nervous and blotchy and forget my lines.

"You go in," Lisa continued, "stand on your mark, and deliver your lines to the camera. Don't worry, I'll be in there to read with you." Somehow knowing that didn't make me worry any less. "And that's all you do, OK? I don't want any procrastination, no preamble, and certainly none of that chit-chat you Brits are so fond of. No one here cares whether or not you can do ballet or tap, or recite Juliet's soliloquy, OK? You do your lines, you move on. Anything that might waste Mr Dubrovnik's very precious time will result in you being automatically disqualified." Lisa Wells paused for a moment to eye each one of us closely, just to make sure she knew we understood her. "Once you've done, I'll show you the way back out to your teacher. I don't want any discussions or giggling going on out here, OK? I want total silence from all of you, except the one who's reading. Any questions?" We all looked at each other, but nobody spoke. Probably because if the others felt anything like I did, they had all lost the power of speech entirely, too.

"Don't worry, girls," Miss Greenstreet said kindly, "I'll be in the café just across the road with a hot chocolate waiting for you when you come out." She shot Lisa Wells her best attempt at a cross look, which wasn't very good because Miss Greenstreet is one of those people who is never actually cross with you, just disappointed. "I'm sure it's not going to be as frightening as you think it is," she said, trying to reassure us.

"Oh, it is," Lisa Wells said, her voice as sharp as her nose.

She scanned her clipboard. "Now, who's first? "Nydia? Which one of you is Nydia?"

Nydia sat perfectly still for a moment as if she hoped that she might blend unnoticed into the orange chair.

"Go on, Nyds," I told her. "You can do—"

"No talking!" Lisa Wells interrupted me. "Nydia, go in now or go home!" Nydia took a deep breath, winked at me and disappeared through the door into the audition room. I scowled surreptitiously at Lisa Wells and wished that I was more like the character I was auditioning to play, Polly Harris aka Ember Buchanen – initially prim and proper, when faced with danger, her character became fearless, cool, calm and collected, even after she finds out that she's not really who she thought she was. In fact, her father isn't her father at all, but an evil historian who kidnapped her as a baby and is planning to murder her on her fourteenth birthday. Polly/Ember was a brave-sassy-no-nonsense-adventurer. She would have just gone up to Lisa Wells and told her what she thought, and quite possibly even kicked her in the shins...

But I, plain old Ruby Parker, did not do any of that, because I never have been any good at rebelling. I just sat on my plastic chair and waited quietly. I watched Nydia, Anne-Marie and the others go in and come out again without even looking at me, until I was the only one left.

"Ruby Parker," Lisa Wells said inevitably. "It's your turn. Go!"

Chapter Two

"Action!"

"I'm sure it wasn't as bad as you think it was," my mum said kindly, putting a steaming bowl of risotto in front of me. It was my favourite comfort food. My mum only ever made it for me on special occasions, or when I was feeling really fed up. I stared at it, feeling the heat coming from it brush against my already flaming cheeks.

"The only way it could have been worse," I told her in a small thin voice, "was if I had actually thrown up *on* Mr Dubrovnik." I screwed up my eyes and felt every internal part of me curl up and shrivel too. I just couldn't believe what had happened. I couldn't believe I had actually been *literally sick* with nerves. *In public.*

"But you read the lines, didn't you?" Mum said, sitting next to me at the kitchen table. "It's not as if you didn't deliver the scene, and I bet you were fabulous."

"I was terrible," I groaned, banging my forehead with the heel of my hands. "Like a five-year-old in a nativity play."

My cat Everest had hauled himself up on to the table top and was eyeing my risotto hopefully. Normally Mum would have shooed him off the table, but he was taking advantage of her concern over me and edged a little bit closer.

"Well, you finished the scene and that's the main thing," my mum said unconvincingly. "And remember, we said it wasn't the end of the world if you didn't get the part. All we have to do is work out what made you feel so terrible and make sure it doesn't happen again next time." I closed my eyes and forced myself to replay the scene one more time.

I had walked into the room, which was much bigger than I had expected, with many more people in it. It was a large room with whitewashed brick walls and a dusty wooden floor. Three sides of the room were lined with floor to ceiling mirrors and ballet bars. Maybe that was what made my nerves worse. Maybe because it seemed like there were thirty people there instead of just ten. Maybe because I could see myself from all of my not-so-brilliant angles.

Or it could have been the camera. After all those years on a soap I didn't think the camera would freak me out at all, but I was wrong. It wasn't the same kind of camera I was used to working with on *Kensington*

Heights: big and clunky and friendly. It was just a digital camcorder on a spindly tripod. I knew exactly how I looked and sounded on a digital camcorder from when my dad sent a home videotape into *Before They Were Famous* a couple of years earlier. I was furious because I looked terrible – dumpy and awkward – and my voice sounded all stupid and high and not at all like it sounded in my head.

I had made myself look at Mr Dubrovnik, who was sitting in the middle of a row of four people, a man who was a bit older than my dad but with longish sandy hair and the kind of clothes I would have thought were far too young and trendy for my dad. And he was wearing a baseball cap, indoors, so I couldn't really see his eyes. But his face was pointed in my direction and he seemed to be the only one of them looking actually *at* me. All the others were looking at a monitor that was showing them how I looked on digital camcorder. Which was rubbish.

I stood on my mark and waited for what seemed like ages before I remembered that Lisa had told us just to read without waiting to be cued.

"I don't know who..." I began my first line just as Mr Dubrovnik spoke.

"You may begin," he said at exactly the same time.

"Er, s... sorry," I told him, stumbling over my words.

"It's just that she said that I…" I trailed off as I remembered what else Lisa had said about "chit-chat". I took a deep breath and looked right down the barrel of the camera.

"I don't know who you think you are!" I more or less shouted my first line.

"I'm your sister, Ember. Don't you remember me at all?" Lisa replied, reading from the script completely deadpan without a trace of emotion. I struggled to stay in character, which was hard, as I felt like I was trying to have a heated argument with someone who expressed about as much emotion as a pre-recorded answerphone message.

"You!" I exclaimed haughtily. "You're not my sister! I'm Polly Harris, daughter of Professor Darkly Harris – the chief curator of the British Museum."

"No. No, you're not," Lisa continued as if she were reading the back of a packet of cornflakes. "You're my little sister and you were stolen from our parents when you were just a baby. I've been searching for you all these years and now at last I've found you."

The flatter and more disinterested Lisa's voice seemed, the more over-the-top and loud my acting became. I knew I was bad, but it was like being at the top of a rollercoaster: I couldn't stop myself from plunging further and further down into over-the-top acting.

"You're lying!" I cried out so loudly my voice rang in my ears and echoed off the painted brick walls.

I did get to the end of my scene without forgetting any lines, that was true. I felt my legs shaking and my stomach wobbling and I delivered the last line with everything I had.

"GET AWAY FROM ME!" I shrieked so loudly I think the mirrors shook.

The sound of my own voice ringing in my ears gradually died away, and when it was gone there was complete silence.

And that was when I threw up. On my feet. On digital camcorder. In front of Hollywood's hottest and most influential director and his entourage. I was as sick as Everest choking up a mammoth-sized hairball.

I don't even know where it came from; it wasn't as if I'd had anything to eat that morning. But suddenly, without any warning, I was bent over double and my stomach was heaving, and I heard this horrible rasping sound and realised it was coming from me.

I didn't wait for Lisa Wells to show me out. I clamped my hand over my mouth and ran out of there as fast as I could, and when I was finally outside I collapsed against the first bit of wall I could find. I stood there for

a moment, my forehead grazing the brick, and I waited until I could breathe steadily and the pavement stopped shifting beneath my feet.

I would have liked to have stayed there all day but I knew I had to go back to the café where the others were waiting. Laughing probably, and talking excitedly without a care in the world because none of them, I was fairly certain, had finished their audition in the same way I had. With retching.

"How did it go?" Nydia exclaimed when she saw me. The whole table stared at me, and I realised that the stricken look on my face might be giving the overall picture of how it went but had failed to fill in the necessary details.

"Bad," I managed to say as I scraped back the remaining empty chair they had been saving for me. "Really bad."

"No, it didn't! I'm sure it didn't," Miss Greenstreet said kindly, patting the back of my hand. "I'm sure you were wonderful. I'm sure that all of you girls were just wonderful."

It was then that I burst into tears.

"So remember what we said?" Mum said, picking up my fork, piling it high with risotto and then aiming it at my mouth. She did this, my mum, sometimes: when things were especially difficult, she'd forget the intervening twelve years and ten months since my birth and treat me like a baby again, even down to spoon-feeding me. I looked at the fork and then at her, and she laid it back in the bowl.

"What did we say?" she said gently, refusing to let go of babying me completely.

"That it's not the end of the world," I recited, seriously unconvinced.

"Because you did your best, didn't you? And that's all you can do, isn't it?" Mum added in the slow, soft voice she used to comfort me with when I grazed my knees.

"I know," I said darkly.

"And there will be other chances," Mum said. "Lots of them."

"Yes," I said heavily. "There will be other chances."

"And after all," Mum seemed determined to wade on through her pep talk despite my total failure to be pepped up by it, "you have to get used to lows as well as highs if you want to be an..."

"An actor!" I snapped. "Yes, I do know, Mum!" I sighed and slumped in my chair, pushing my bowl of risotto away from me so that it slid to a stop by Everest's neat little paws. He licked his lips.

There was no point in being angry with Mum. She wasn't the one who had messed up the audition so badly that it could well go into the number one slot of the Top Ten All-Time Most Messed-up Auditions Chart.

"I'm sorry, Mum," I said. "It's just, well, I know all about taking rejection and getting used to it and picking myself up and dusting myself off and getting ready for the next challenge; we have classes on it at school. After all, one of the reasons I left *Kensington Heights* was so that I could experience all of that – stretch myself, find new challenges. But, well... I suppose I didn't expect it to happen to me. Not really." I chewed at my bottom lip. "Maybe it means that I can't act. Maybe I'm really rubbish, after all. I only ever really played myself in *Kensington Heights*."

It was true. When I left the show, my character Angel was a quite shy, not very popular and ever-so-slightly-dumpy thirteen-year-old – and so was I. I thought that if I played another character, one like Polly Harris, I might change too. I should have known it wouldn't be that easy.

"Ruby, you are not rubbish," Mum said, using her old no-nonsense voice again. "You are wonderful! Look, you had one bad audition – it's not..."

"The end of the world," I finished for her, suddenly wishing more than anything that it was because anything – even an apocalypse – would be preferable to having to go to school in the morning.

HIYA! BYE-A!

Issue number 00234   RRP £1.75

IN THIS ISSUE:

The newest cast member of

THE DENTISTS –

TATIANA KHAN

– shows us round her country retreat.

BRIT BRATS!

The rise and rise of the young British talent that's taking the rest of the world by storm. We talk to

DANNY HARVEY

about what it means to be young, British and talented.

PLUS

ALL THE LATEST ENTERTAINMENT GOSSIP

HOW TO HAVE HAIR LIKE IMOGENE GRANT'S

YOUR STARS

AND MUCH, MUCH MORE!

ISBN –hiyabiya–234
9 00234 £1.75 >

Chapter Three

"Action!"

"Oh, shut up, Menakshi,"
Anne-Marie said as we
walked back in from netball
practice the next day, dogged by Menakshi Shah and Jade
Caruso, who had been compulsively teasing me since news
got round about my terrible audition. "What do you know
anyway?" Anne-Maire snapped at them. "Neither of you
two were even good enough to get into the first audition."

"Well, we should have been," Menakshi said sharply.
"At least I wouldn't have chucked up everywhere – in
front of Art Dubrovnik! Not quite as professional as you
think, are you, Ruby? What's it like being one of the
crowd again now you've had your fifteen minutes of
fame? Ready for a lifetime of lame?" She and Jade
cackled like a pair of witches.

"Well, at least her fifteen minutes was in a top-rated
soap and not in a nit commercial, Jade," Nydia said,
joining us from the bench where she had been first sub
again. "And it was much longer than fifteen minutes that
Ruby was famous for."

Jade laughed. "Peaked too soon, that's your trouble," she teased me. "For the rest of us things can only get better; for you it's downhill all the way. Career over at thirteen – what a shame."

"Jade." Anne-Marie stepped in front of the other girl so that her pretty little nose was about two millimetres from Jade's, and she snarled at her like a tiger. "I told you to shut up, all right?" For a moment Anne-Marie showed all her old qualities that Nydia and I had known and feared last school year, back when she had been our mortal enemy. I never thought we would end up being friends, but it was just before I decided to leave *Kensington Heights*, and I had just found out I had this kiss scene with Justin de Souza, who I used to really, really fancy. I had never kissed anybody before in my life, so I sort of panicked, and Nydia said the only thing to do was to get training from someone who definitely had kissing experience. And the only person we knew who definitely had kissing experience was Anne-Marie. We had to bribe her to help us, and even then it was extremely scary, very emotional and rather dramatic. And somehow at the end of all that the three of us ended up as best friends. Which meant it was easy to forget that Anne-Marie could still be totally ruthless, completely hard and the fastest insult-hurler in the school when she wanted to be. I was relieved that she was our friend now instead of our mortal enemy. They seemed like much more appealing characteristics to have in a friend, especially when I had Menakshi and Jade crowing in my face.

"One more word and..." Anne-Marie said in a low, soft voice. She didn't have to add anything else to the sentence. Just her tone made Jade and Menakshi fall back into their pack to carry out further bitching at a safe distance, while the three of us stalked across the fields towards the academy.

"Thanks," I said to Anne-Marie.

"No worries," Anne-Marie said, all sunshine and smiles again. "Look, everybody will stop talking about it soon, won't they, Nyds?"

"Yes," Nydia said, dropping her arm round my shoulders and giving me a squeeze. "Soon no one will be interested in you at all. I mean they will," she added hastily. "But in a good way." I lifted my chin and made myself smile at my two friends.

"It's OK anyway," I lied. "I'm fine about it now, really I am. I don't care any more at all. Not a bit. And I'm the one that messed up. There's a really good chance that you two might get called back for a second audition. So I'm rooting for you two now. As long as one of us three gets it then it will be brilliant!"

I didn't feel as upbeat as I sounded but I didn't want to spoil it for Anne-Marie and Nydia, making them walk on egg shells around me, pretending that they didn't mind either way if they got a part in a Hollywood movie.

"Really?" Anne-Marie asked me, jumping on my words. "Oh, good, because I've been *dying* to show you two this." She dug into the pocket of her gym skirt and brought out a folded-up clipping. "It's from *Hiya! Bye-a!*" she said, referring to her favourite celebrity magazine. "It's about the film, Ruby. I didn't want to make you feel bad by looking at it in front of you and it felt wrong to look at it behind your back, but if you really are OK... You sure you don't mind us looking at it?"

I made myself laugh happily. If only I had been this good at acting during the audition.

"Of course not!" I said cheerily.

She handed me the clipping and I unfolded it. The title read: "Imogene shouts 'Action!' for her next big role."

"You read it out," I said, handing the piece of paper to Nydia. She took it eagerly and scanned the text.

"Casting is almost complete for the new Imogene Grant blockbuster *The Lost Treasure of King Arthur.*" Anne-Marie and Nydia looked at each other with bright eyes. "Veteran action hero Harry McLean is confirmed as the male lead, and also starring will be... Oh my gosh!" Nydia said, sounding suddenly breathless.

"I know," Anne-Marie squealed. "Read it out! Read it out!"

I looked from one girl to the other. They both looked like they might explode.

"And also starring will be Hollywood's hottest teen heart-throb *Sean Rivers!*"

"Arrrrrrgh!" the two girls screamed in unison and danced around me in a little circle.

"Sean Rivers, Ruby! Only Sean Rivers!" Nydia exclaimed. "Oh my gosh!"

I smiled at both of them. It was starting to hurt.

"Wow," I said, the edge in my voice floating over the tops of the heads of my two friends. "Sean Rivers. *The* Sean Rivers. We totally *love* him."

"Just think..." Anne-Marie said, hooking her arm though mine as we approached the changing rooms. "One of *us* could be working with Sean Rivers, the very same *Sean Rivers* we all went to see in *A Cheerleader's Destiny.*"

"And *Last Summer's Love*," Nydia added wistfully.

"And *The Underdogs*," Anne-Marie said. "Oh, he was so lovely in *The Underdogs* – that bit when he thought he might not be able to play in the final because of his leg and he cried...?"

"Oh my gosh, I love him," Nydia added sincerely.

"*I* love him," Anne-Marie said.

"I love him more," Nydia said with a giggle.

"Who loves who more?" Danny said, jogging up to us in his football kit. He had a big smear of mud across his nose, and I have never been so pleased to see my normal lovely real-life boyfriend before in my life. My smile for him was a real one as he dropped his arm around my shoulders and raised a dark eyebrow at the girls.

"Don't tell me you're going out with Michael Henderson again?" he asked Anne-Marie, who made a sour face at the mention of her ex-boyfriend's name.

"Read this." Nydia handed Danny the now grubby clipping and he read it quickly.

"And?" he asked, looking mystified.

"Sean Rivers!" Nydia exclaimed. "We all love him." She gestured at the three of us.

"I don't," I said, looking at Danny fondly.

"Oh yeah, so why has she got that poster of him over her bed then, hey, Danny?" Anne-Marie said, teasing me gently.

Danny shrugged.

"Has she?" he said. "I hadn't noticed." He neglected

to mention that in fact he'd never been in my bedroom because my mum wouldn't let him go in there with me unless we were accompanied by at least three adult chaperones.

Still, Danny was determined to be unimpressed by Sean Rivers, and I knew it was partly because he was worrying about how I was feeling after blowing my chances of ever meeting him, let alone working with him. Knowing that made me feel a lot better. Even almost happy.

"These two are going all gooey at the thought of actually *possibly* meeting him," I said with a laugh, to show him that I didn't mind talking about the film.

"Over Sean Rivers?" Danny mocked them. "He's just a bloke, you know. Like me."

Nydia and Anne-Marie screeched with overexcited laughter, and Danny's face coloured a little.

"A bloke who's got millions of fans all round the world!" Anne-Marie said.

"Yeah," Danny said a little defensively. "Like me."

"Like you!" Anne-Marie hooted, and even I couldn't hide my smile.

"Yeah, like me," Danny said. "I *am* on Britain's favourite soap, you know. Last month I got as many fan letters as Justin."

That shut us all up. None of us had known that before.

"You got as many letters as Justin de Souza?" I stared hard at Danny. Yes, he was still the same normal lovely real-life boyfriend I had five minutes ago. But Justin? Everybody knew that Justin got hundreds of fan letters nearly every month.

"Hang on," I said. "You mean problem letters like I used to get, don't you?"

Danny seemed to consider his answer for a moment, but then he looked at Nydia and Anne-Marie's bright laughing faces and said, with a hint of pride, "No, I mean I get actual 'I love you, Danny' fan letters. Not that they mean anything at all," he added quickly.

"Of course," I said, checking back on my mum's criteria for what constituted the end of the world. If stupendously fluffing the most important audition I would probably ever have didn't count, would finding out that my normal lovely real-life boyfriend was now the object of affection for thousands – maybe millions – of girls, sixty per cent of whom at *least* would be thinner and prettier than me, qualify?

"We'll be late for English," I said, shrugging Danny's arm off my shoulders and heading for the refuge of the girls' changing room.

I didn't want to react that way. I wanted to laugh it off and say something witty and funny about how of course he had loads of fans, he was my boyfriend, wasn't he? But I couldn't. I suddenly felt cross and jealous all over, and I just wanted to go somewhere Danny wasn't until I could feel normal again.

"Ruby!" Danny called out after me as I marched off.

"Don't worry," I heard Nydia say as I went through the door. "She's just having a bad day, that's all."

By the time we had filed into the classroom, I had given myself a good talking to, washed the frown off my face and brushed the irritation out of my hair. It wasn't my friends' fault that they did well at the audition and I didn't. It wasn't Danny's fault that he was really good in *Kensington Heights* and very photogenic, causing swathes of young girls to dream about him. I shouldn't be jealous, I should feel lucky. Lucky I have such talented friends and such a great boyfriend. If a year ago, when I was so unpopular I only had one friend and I was officially the least likely girl in the academy and quite possibly the world to ever have a boyfriend, I could have seen myself now – in with the in-crowd (mostly) and with Danny on my arm – I would have thought I had reached the pinnacle of happiness. But I knew it wasn't really those three that I was angry with – it was myself; I was furious with myself.

Try as I might I couldn't help going back over and over my twenty minutes in front of Mr Dubrovnik, replaying and replaying them until I finally got it right, until I was brilliant and triumphant and he jumped up from his seat and offered me the part on the spot. And for a few short moments I would feel enormous relief, until I remembered it was only a daydream. A lot of things have happened over the past year, things that I would rather hadn't happened. Mainly Mum and Dad deciding to separate. But even then, even when it came down to my parents splitting up, I sort of knew deep down, through all the anger and the hurt, that it had to happen; that that was the way it had to be. Mum said so often enough since it had happened. I can't say it doesn't hurt at all any more; it does. But I feel like I can live with it.

But what happened at the audition was not scripted. It wasn't supposed to be like that at all, and the only person I could blame for it going wrong was me. And there was nothing I could do to change it.

That moment had been for real and not just a

rehearsal. It was a chance that had gone for ever, and knowing that stung, like a hard cold slap. Mum was right; I hoped there would be other auditions, other chances, but that one would never come round again.

Danny was already sitting at his desk as I walked in. I offered him a small apologetic shrug.

"I'm sorry," I said. "I don't know what came over me."

"It's all right," he said, pulling out a chair so I could sit next to him. "You're having a bad day. I know you feel bad about that audition, but you're brilliant, Ruby. If you don't get it, it's because something bigger and better is waiting for you." I smiled at him as I sat down, and he picked up my hand. "And look, those fan letters are really nothing. Look, here's one I got this morning. I haven't even opened it yet. You open it." I knew I should have said, "Oh, don't be so silly," but I nodded and took the letter and opened it. The handwriting was large and round and some of the words weren't exactly spelt right.

Dear Danny from the TV,

   I think you are really brilyant and good in kensinton heights. You are my favourite and mummy lets me stay up until nine o clock when its on to see you because you are so good. She

37

said I could write in and join a fan club if
I wanted because you are really good. Please
can I have a signed photo. I have a rabbit
called Danny too.

Thank you very much

Love from

kirsty Green aged six and a half and a bit

"Oh bless!" I said, handing the letter to Danny.
"That's so cute that little girls like you!"

"Yeah, well," Danny said, "I told you. I mean not
all of them are from six-year-olds, obviously, and
even if some of them do go on about fancying me, it
doesn't make a difference to us. You do know that, don't
you?"

I nodded. "Of course I do," I said.

"Because it would be stupid to get jealous over a load
of letters," Danny said.

"I *know*," I said. "And I'm not jealous any more."

"Before we begin..." Miss Greenstreet stood at the front
of the class in her long gypsy skirt, bouncing on the balls
of her feet. That meant only one thing – Shakespeare. She
only ever bounced when we read Shakespeare. She said
once that she loved teaching English at the academy
because at least when students read aloud in class they

sounded like they meant it. Once Menakshi and Michael read the death scene in *Romeo and Juliet* and Miss Greenstreet actually cried. I don't know why – it wasn't *that* good.

"Class!" Miss Greenstreet raised her voice a little, and the chattering settled and quietened. "Two of you will be excused from class today because Ms Lighthouse wants to see you in her office immediately."

"It wasn't me!" Michael Henderson shouted from the back of the class. A few of the boys sniggered and laughed.

"Actually, Michael, it's not because of something someone's done wrong. It's because of something two other people have done right." Miss Greenstreet lowered her voice a little and smiled. "I'm not supposed to say anything, but I *think* it's about the auditions for Mr Dubrovnik." Anne-Marie and Nydia looked at each other and gripped hands tightly. "So," Miss Greenstreet said, smiling broadly, "can Anne-Marie and Ruby go to Ms Lighthouse's office right away, please?"

Anne-Marie, who had jumped up at the sound of her name, sat down heavily again.

"It's the brush-off," Menakshi called from behind me. "She's telling the losers first that they haven't got through. Hey, Nydia, you might be getting a call back!"

Nydia said nothing, but looked from me to Anne-Marie. Anne-Marie stood up again, the sparkle and smile gone from her face. She knew that to be called with me meant rejection.

"Come on," she said. "We might as well go and get it over with."

Miss Greenstreet smiled at us as we headed for the door.

"You never know, girls, it might be good news," she said. But neither one of us replied.

"I really thought I was good," Anne-Marie said as we trudged towards Ms Lighthouse's office.

"You were good," I said. "I was the terrible one."

"Exactly," Anne-Marie said.

Ms Lighthouse's office door was open and her assistant Mrs Moore nodded for us to go in. It was hard to tell what kind of news we were going to get from Mrs Moore's expression, as never once had anyone ever seen her smile, frown or have any kind of expression at all. She was permanently in neutral, with a face like a mask that might hide thousands of raging thoughts and emotions.

"Sit," Sylvia Lighthouse commanded us as we walked into her office, and we obeyed promptly. She leaned forward across her desk on her elbows and examined each one of us carefully before sitting back in her chair.

"Well, well," she said, more to herself than to us. "Cometh the hour, cometh the girls."

"Huh?" Anne-Marie and I said together.

"Action!"

Chapter Four

"But – are you sure?" I said, quite unable to believe what Sylvia Lighthouse had just told Anne-Marie and me. "Because I was really terrible."

"I wasn't," Anne-Marie said. "I was great."

Sylvia read aloud again the fax she had in her hand.

" 'Dear Ms Lighthouse,'" she read, affecting a gruff New York accent. "'Thank you for sending your young ladies to audition for the part of Polly Harris in *The Lost Treasure of King Arthur*. There are two that interested me and whom I'd like to see again this Friday: Ruby Parker and Anne-Marie Chance. Details to follow.'" Sylvia Lighthouse put the fax down on the table and looked at us.

"He wants to see you two again," she said. "This time it will be a longer audition. You'll read through a scene chosen by Mr Dubrovnik that you won't get to rehearse before you arrive, and I know he sometimes likes to get actors doing improvisation work, to see who has the right 'chemistry'. You might have to do some of that."

Anne-Marie and I looked at each other.

"Um…" I said, not quite able to believe what I was about to say, "Ms Lighthouse, I think he's got me mixed up with someone else – Nydia maybe? Because I… threw up in my audition. In front of him." Ms Lighthouse raised her eyebrows and wrinkled her long nose.

"Well, Ruby, he doesn't say he thought you were *good*. He says he thought you were *interesting*. He has not made a mistake. Mr Dubrovnik is not the sort of man to make mistakes." She tapped her nails on the desk and looked at us. "Now, as I understand, there are three other girls from other 'sources' also going to this second call-back, so the chances of you progressing further are slim. Nevertheless, shooting is due to begin within the month, so we need to assume the impossible and talk practicalities with your parents."

"Mine are in South Africa," Anne-Marie said, and then, after a moment, "and Canada. Dad's in Canada."

I glanced at Anne-Marie. Usually the fact that her movie-producer dad and fashionista mum were more often abroad on business than at home didn't seem to bother her too much. But sometimes, like just at that moment, you could see her bravado drop a little, and you got a tiny glimpse of sadness. Most of the school thought she had the best time ever, living in her big posh house with only her older brother and their housekeeper Pilar to look after her. But I knew that sometimes, just sometimes, Anne-Marie would like nothing more than to be grounded by one or preferably both of her parents, just as long as they were at home.

"Very well. I'll need contact numbers then – and, Ruby, I'll phone your mother and father separately. They will both need to consent."

"OK," I said. It still felt strange that they had separate home phone numbers.

"For whoever gets the part of Polly Harris it will be an intensive six-week shoot. Child working laws still apply, of course, so it does mean that if either of you two get the part, you would be taken out of school for the remainder of this term and taught on set by a specially provided tutor, who will know your curriculum and will make sure you do not fall behind with your school work." Ms Lighthouse gave us one of her brief twitches of a smile. "You will also need an adult guardian with you at all times."

"I don't think either of my parents will be able to do

that," Anne-Marie said, looking a little downcast. "I don't think we've spent six weeks in one place together ever in my life."

"Well," Ms Lighthouse said. "If needs be, Anne-Marie, I'll chaperone you myself. I won't have you missing out on a chance like this. So don't you worry about *that*." She gave Anne-Marie one of her brief, rare, full-length smiles.

"Now, you two must focus on Friday. Ruby, you suffered terribly from nerves the last time. I want you to harness those nerves; make them work for you. Don't let anything knock you off course again. Mr Dubrovnik must have seen something in you to make him want to see you again. Try and think what that might have been and give it a chance to really shine. Anne-Marie, you are a lovely-looking girl, but don't rely on good looks to get you through this. Mr Dubrovnik may be shooting an action film, but he wants actors in it, not mannequins. He hasn't won two Oscars just for casting pretty faces. You have talent, make sure you use it." Anne-Marie and I nodded, and then I thought of Nydia sitting in English class still thinking that she might have got called back.

"Excuse me, Ms Lighthouse," I asked her. "Does that mean no one else from the academy is going back?"

"I'm afraid so," she said, looking at her watch. "I want you to go to the library for the remainder of your lesson until lunch break. I'll be seeing those other girls now." She studied mine and Anne-Marie's faces for a moment and I could guess what she saw there. I hardly knew myself how I felt.

"Don't feel bad about it, girls," she said, her voice unexpectedly softened. "This is what acting is about. Sometimes seeing your friends fail means that you have succeeded."

Mrs Moore watched us as we filed out of Sylvia Lighthouse's office and turned right towards the library. Then she left her desk and began walking steadily to fetch the other girls who hadn't made it through. The other girls including Nydia.

"Poor Nydia," I whispered to Anne-Marie as we sat over open books that we had plucked from the shelves without even reading the title. I wanted to run about and scream and laugh, but given that we had been sent to the library all of those things were impossible. So instead we had to sit and wait until we could tell everyone else – tell Nydia.

"I know," Anne-Marie said. "But you heard what she said, she said don't feel bad because—"

"I know," I said. "But I don't want it to be like that, do you? I don't want to be that competitive. And friends you count on, friends like Nydia and you, are really important. I don't ever want to see a friend fail so that I can succeed."

"But did you honestly feel like that this morning before you knew you had been called back?" Anne-Marie asked me. I shrugged, but said nothing. She was right, though. If I was really, really honest, this morning a part of me had hoped that none of us would get the part so we could all go back to being normal again. It was only now that I knew I was getting called back that I truly wished Nydia was coming too.

"Look, Ruby," Anne-Marie whispered, "acting is one big competition. And somehow, by some amazing miracle, you – Ruby Parker – are one of the winners at the moment. And that's all you've got to think about right now. I know that's all I'm thinking about. And Nydia will be happy for us; like you said, she is a good friend."

I stared blankly at the pages of words in front of me without reading them.

Somehow the impossible had happened. Somehow I *had* done something right, something that meant I was going to get another chance to impress Mr Dubrovnik, to get the part of Polly Harris. I didn't know what I had done or how I had done it, but I did know one thing: I was going to give the best performance of my life.

This time, I was going to be brilliant.

Chapter Five

"Action!"

The Waldorf Hotel in
London was the poshest
place I had ever been to in my life. OK, I haven't been to
that many posh places unless you count award
ceremonies, and they are usually held in a theatre or TV
studio, which aren't nearly as posh as they look on TV.

"This is the life, hey, Ruby?" Dad said, winking as we
waited in the foyer for Mr Dubrovnik to call us up, with
my mum, Anne-Marie and Sylvia Lighthouse herself,
who had decided to replace Miss Greenstreet on this
occasion as it was "a matter of academy honour".

"Totally," I said, looking around me at the gold and
the mirrors and the soft chair and posh orange ladies
with big hair and big sunglasses and heavy-looking
jewellery.

"Frank!" My mum looked as nervous as I felt. "Try
not to look like a tourist."

"It's a hotel," Dad said, shrugging and grinning at
me. "It's built for tourists, hey, Rube?" I laughed because

I knew he was trying to make me laugh, thinking it would take my mind off my nerves. And in a way it did, because the two of them being here together reassured me and made me feel safe again in a way that just one of them, try as they might, could not.

It was great that Mum and Dad had decided that both of them were coming with me to this important audition. And I was glad that they'd had a long phone conversation about it, a conversation during which no one had raised their voice or slammed down the receiver (or in our case pressed the "End Call" button really firmly). And I was really glad when Mum had come into the living room where I had been earwigging and said, "I suppose you heard, Dad's coming too on Friday. So that'll be nice, won't it?"

That seemed to be like a big step to me, part of the general air of friendship that had gradually begun to build between them since that horrible night when Dad left us and it had seemed as if nothing would be right in our family again. OK, they were living apart and Dad had his so-called "girlfriend". And yes, Mum had cut her hair and started wearing make-up to go to the supermarket. Not to mention arranging sleepovers for me so she could go to salsa classes with her friends, who as it turned out she had a lot more of than I realised. But, I decided, as strange and as uncomfortable as some of that made me feel, it didn't matter as long as they were talking to each other and not hating each other, and sometimes when it was really important I could have both of them together again looking after me. I couldn't have them back together again but I knew this was the next best thing.

Anne-Marie crossed the polished marble floor to my side and grinned at me.

"Well," she said, "how are you feeling?" I paused to listen for any early-warning gurgle from my tummy.

"Strangely OK," I said, sounding slightly surprised. "You?"

"I'm OK," she said, biting her glossy lip. "It was sweet of Nydia to call us this morning and wish us good luck, wasn't it?" she said. "Good old Nydia, she's been really great about this, hasn't she?"

"Yes," I said, although I hadn't spoken to Nydia that morning or the night before. Perhaps she had called home just after I'd left. Or maybe she'd been trying my mobile, which Sylvia had made us turn off before we came into the hotel.

"You can come up now." Lisa Wells appeared as if from nowhere and spoke so loudly that the posh orange people stopped to look at her from over the tops of their morning papers. At the sound of her voice I felt my stomach tighten and gurgle.

"You can do this, love," Dad said. "You're the best, remember that!" I nodded as our little group headed for the lift.

"We have two suites reserved – one for waiting in, the other for a brief rehearsal with a member of the cast and then the screen test. Ruby, you're going in first, so less chance for you to inflate the hotel's extra cleaning charges, and Anne-Marie, you'll be waiting in the second suite. There will be refreshments while you wait. It won't take long – a little over half an hour, I think. Then you'll go in, Anne-Marie, and Ruby can wait. Is that OK, girls?"

"That will be perfectly fine," Ms Lighthouse said before either of us could open our mouths.

At first I sort of wished I had been in a suite at the Waldorf Hotel for some reason other than auditioning for a part in the new film of world-famous movie director Art Dubrovnik. Then I could have enjoyed it even more.

The waiting suite was amazing: the biggest bedroom I have ever seen in my life. In fact, you couldn't really call it a bedroom, it was more like an apartment, with a huge living room, bathroom and even an *upstairs*. Of course, Anne-Marie swanked around like she spent her whole life in hotel rooms like this one, and given that her mum and dad were in the top fifty richest people in the country, she probably had. I on the other hand was awestruck and so were my parents, although my mum didn't look around the room open-mouthed with awe like my dad did, she sat still on the edge of the blue silk sofa and looked afraid to touch anything.

"I'll be right back," Lisa said, her eye raking over Anne-Maire and me again. "There's tea and fresh coffee over there, or take what you like from the minibar as long as it's legal." As Sylvia Lighthouse busied herself pouring coffee and tea for my parents, Anne-Marie crossed straight to a part of the wall that I had thought was just white-painted wooden panelling and opened it to reveal a tiny but well-stocked fridge.

She handed me a Coke and took one for herself.

"How did you know that was there?" I asked her, impressed.

"It was obvious," she said. "Minibars are always in the same place, aren't they?" I said nothing and went and sat next to my mum and sipped my drink. Sylvia Lighthouse was talking but I wasn't listening. All I could think about was that it was me who would be going to audition first. I knew that it was going to happen, but I couldn't quite believe it. Somehow it didn't seem real. It felt like I was already playing a part in a film.

"OK." Lisa Wells opened the door. "Ruby, come this way, please."

I looked at my mum, who smiled at me and nodded, and then at my dad, who pumped his fist in the air in a way that would have ordinarily mortified me if I hadn't been so nervous, and then finally at Sylvia Lighthouse, who was standing straight-backed against the window.

"Remember everything I've taught you and you will excel," she told me with quiet dignity.

"I will, Ms Lighthouse," I said solemnly, though to be perfectly honest at that point I couldn't remember a single word she had ever said about anything ever. I could hardly even remember my name.

"We are working to a schedule here, you know," Lisa Wells said, rolling her eyes. I stood up and I followed her into the second suite.

Mr Dubrovnik was sitting on a fat, cream sort of half-sofa half-chair, leaning forward with his elbows resting on his knees as if at any moment he might want to suddenly get up and leave. He watched me as I walked in through the door and pointed at the chair opposite him.

"Hello, Ruby," he said. His voice was soft and low and quite friendly really.

"Hello," I said. My voice was high and squeaky and sounded quite a lot like a strangulated mouse.

"Well, I'm glad to see you again," Mr Dubrovnik said. "I bet you didn't think you'd be asked back, did you?" I shook my head. It seemed like a better alternative than squeaky-voiced talking. Mr Dubrovnik smiled. He had a very nice fatherly sort of smile that wrinkled his face up around his eyes and made him look about a hundred times less scary.

"And so, Ruby, why do you think I've asked you to come to this second audition today?" he asked. I thought about it for a moment and realised that this time I'd have to speak, so I concentrated on making my voice come out as normal as possible.

"Well," I said, and this time I still sounded like a mouse but not one who had been breathing the helium from party balloons, "I thought you might have got me mixed up with another Ruby." It was a terrible answer, but the only one I had, and I was rewarded with another one of Mr Dubrovnik's friendly smiles. He laughed and shook his head.

"So you thought you did pretty badly, right?" he said, twinkling at me. I found myself smiling back at him as I nodded.

"Well, I'll tell you," he said. "You did. You *were* terrible. You let the situation rule you, and an actor can never, *never* allow that to happen. You have to rule the situation at all times. No matter how difficult it is. You have to *own* it. You'll learn that if you ever work in live theatre." I nodded.

"I have done live theatre," I said quickly. "School plays." Mr Dubrovnik laughed again and this time so did I. I had no idea that I was so hilarious. His face settled into a smile again and he leaned even further forward in his chair as if he were about to tell me a secret.

"I'll tell you why you're here, Ruby, and I won't lie," he told me. "You've got something none of the other girls going for this part have got." I held my breath, hoping he was about to say something like "real talent", but instead he said, "You've got history and years of experience. I've seen the show you were in, *Kensington Lofts*, or whatever." I nodded. "I asked Sylvia to send me over some tapes after your first audition because I couldn't believe that the performance you gave was really your best." I shook my head with emphasis. "Thought not, so I watched about four episodes and – you were really good in it. *Really* good considering those scripts." He smiled again; it was a smile that seemed to reach right up to his forehead. "Also, you might like to know that Miss Grant liked your audition. She said she thought you had something about you that might be right for the part." I thought how nice that this Miss Grant, whoever she might be, liked me, and then I realised who he was talking about! Not just *a* Miss Grant, but *the* Miss Grant – Imogene Grant!

"Imogene Grant thought that from seeing the tape of my audition?" I said, sounding incredulous. "Did she see that last bit?" I asked him, mortified. He smiled.

"Afraid so," he said. I clapped my hands over my eyes and he laughed again.

"Yeah, I know," Art Dubrovnik said. "But even with the last bit, she wanted me to see you again and I'm not in the habit of saying no to my leading lady. So are you all set?"

I took a deep breath.

"As I'll ever be," I said.

Mr Dubrovnik nodded.

"Jeremy!" he called out to another room most politely. "Would you mind coming through now, please?" And my jaw dropped as Britain's leading thespian and one of the world's top film actors walked into the room. It was Jeremy Fort.

"Hello," he said to me, giving me a little bow.

"My mum so *loves* you," I said to him without thinking, and then they were both laughing. I felt myself flush red to the roots of my hair, which may have been a blessing in disguise because at least then they couldn't see the blotches I was coming out in.

"I can see you know who Jeremy is," Art Dubrovnik said. "He will be playing Polly's 'father' – the evil scientist who kidnaps her." He handed me a script bound in a dark blue cover. "Here's a short scene for you to learn. I want you to spend a few minutes learning your lines with Jeremy and then I'll come back into the room and you give me your best shot, OK?"

I couldn't speak; I was too busy praying my breakfast wouldn't want to make another cameo appearance.

"Ruby," Mr Dubrovnik said, gently but firmly, his smile settling in the bottom half of his face only. "If you want to act, you can't be star-struck. You have to act like you're just as important as anyone else in this room; you have to *own* this room, OK?" I nodded, and tried not to think about the fact that I barely had enough pocket money to own a box of complimentary matches, let alone anything else in this room.

"OK, I'll try," I managed to say, and then as I looked at Mr Dubrovnik's encouraging smile spreading back past his eyebrows, I remembered what I had forgotten the first time. That this was my chance, my one chance to get it right and to at least do the best I could do, so that this afternoon and tomorrow and next week I wouldn't be kicking myself, wishing again and again that I'd done things differently. This was my moment. I had to give it everything I could.

"I'll give it my best shot, Mr Dubrovnik," I said, my voice sounding clear and even again. Mr Dubrovnik looked pleased.

"I look forward to it," he said.

When he had left the room Jeremy Fort looked at me and said, "Now then, Ruby, shall we begin?"

THE LOST TREASURE OF KING ARTHUR©

A WIDE OPEN UNIVERSE PRODUCTION

DIRECTED BY *ART DUBROVNIK*
WRITTEN BY *ART DUBROVNIK* AND *ADRIENNE SCOTT*

STARRING: *IMOGENE GRANT, HARRY MCLEAN* AND *SEAN RIVERS*

INT. DAYTIME – PROFESSOR DARKLY'S OFFICE AT THE BRITISH MUSEUM

The office is lined with shelves of very old-looking books. There is a huge ancient-looking round table covered in scrolls and manuscripts. There is a mummified head on the table. It looks like it died in terrible agony. PROFESSOR DARKLY HARRIS stands with his back to

camera, looking out of the window.
POLLY HARRIS runs into the room to
tell him what CATCHER SMITH has just
told her. She is anxious and out of
breath.

POLLY

Daddy! Daddy! Oh, thank
goodness, there you are.
You have to come quickly.
There's this American boy
downstairs saying terrible
things about you, Daddy!
Terrible lies. He must be
quite mad!

Professor Darkly turns around slowly
and smiles at his "daughter". It's
the dark, deadly smile of a monster
who is preparing to finish off his
prey.

PROFESSOR DARKLY

Now, now, Polly dear. Do
calm down. I'm sure it's

just another tourist
playing some kind of joke.
You know what these
Americans are like. They
have no appreciation of any
real history. Just sit down
and tell me calmly what he
said to you.

POLLY sits reluctantly at the table
on the only free chair. She looks
unhappily at the mummified head. It
seems to be staring right at her.

POLLY
Well, this one knew a lot
about Arthurian legend,
Daddy. He said… he said
that – that you weren't my
father at all! That you had
kidnapped me because I was
a child born on the seventh
hour of the seventh day of
the seventh month, which
made me perfect for your

evil purposes. He said that you were an evil scientist and worse still the direct descendant of the evil sorcerer Mordred. And that you were planning to resurrect the sleeping body of King Arthur and enslave him with a powerful spell, so that he would show you where the sword Excalibur was hidden, thus giving you the power to conquer the world and bring about an apocalypse!

PROFESSOR DARKLY laughs. It is a dark and menacing laugh, one that POLLY has never heard before from her beloved and kindly father. She starts to feel afraid of him but is still disbelieving. Professor Darkly leans menacingly over the table.

PROFESSOR DARKLY

And was there anybody else
with this boy, my dear?

POLLY leans back in her chair.

POLLY

He said… he said he had
come with my sister. My
real sister who had been
looking for me since the
day you took me. He said
her name was Flame
Buchanen.

PROFESSOR DARKLY howls in rage and
sweeps the papers off the round
table. The mummified head falls into
POLLY'S lap. She jumps up and
screams.

PROFESSOR DARKLY

That cursed woman will ruin
everything!

Polly creeps gradually further away
from her father back towards the open
door. She is very afraid and confused.

POLLY

Daddy? What do you mean it
will ruin everything? What
do you mean?

PROFESSOR DARKLY narrows his eyes
and looks at his retreating
daughter. Slowly, slowly he begins
to stalk towards her, a terrible
smile on his face.

PROFESSOR DARKLY

My dear, I had hoped to keep
all this from you until the
last moment. But I suppose
it *is* almost the last
moment. Everything that boy
told you is true. I have
raised you and pretended to
love you. But our entire
life has been a lie - a lie

waiting for this day, this very night! For tonight is the night when the ancient prophecy shall come true at last and King Arthur will walk this earth again, but not as a hero to save the world from destruction. Oh, no, he will be my slave. And to make him my slave I need to make a sacrifice to my forefather Mordred. A *human* sacrifice, my dear. A child born on the seventh hour of the seventh day of the seventh month. A girl descended from Guinevere herself. I think you'll find that's you!

In tears of disbelief and fear POLLY runs towards the open door, but PROFESSOR DARKLY gets there first and slams it shut in her face.

Chapter Six

"Action!"

As we waited for Anne-Marie to come back from the audition suite, I went over and over the last half an hour again and again, just like I had with the first audition.

After about five minutes I had forgotten that Jeremy Fort was Jeremy Fort, and started to think of him as my fellow actor, just in the same way I would have thought of Nydia in the school play or Brett on the show. As we looked at the short but emotional scene, I started to feel just as I used to at work: I felt like I knew what I was doing.

I was wrong though – at least partly.

Jeremy told me that the first read-through of a scene should be to get the rhythm of the words, so as we read our lines to each other I tried my best to do what he said. But he stopped me and reminded me.

"Listen for the rhythm, Ruby; don't turn it into a musical!" I looked at him. I had no time to bluff my way through.

"I don't think I understand you," I said, intently wanting to be able to. Jeremy thought for a moment.

"Ruby," he said eventually. "If you want a career as an actor, you have to be the best of the best. You have to remember that whatever job you are doing, from a toothpaste commercial to a blockbuster movie, you have to treat it as if it were the role of a lifetime – a work of genius that the bard could have written himself. Remember that without your script you are literally nothing. Pay it respect and don't just read it – *listen* to it. Listening to the rhythm of the lines and – even more crucially – to your fellow actors is the single most important skill you will ever learn as an actor. Because whether you and I have read this scene once or a thousand times, when our audience sees it, it must be absolutely fresh and spontaneous. Every single time you hear me say my lines to you, you have to listen to them as if it's for the very first time." Jeremy gave me a small tight smile. "If you can do that – you can do anything."

And when he said that, it was as if I suddenly understood a really long and really difficult maths equation that I had been staring and staring at for hours and hours and was unable to make sense of. It was as if at last I understood this great big secret that everyone else had been in on except for me. In the space of five minutes, Jeremy Fort had given me knowledge that would make me a better actor no matter *how* this audition turned out. And that all by itself nearly made it worth coming here today, whatever the result.

But only nearly, because suddenly – knowing the kind of actors that I would be working with and learning from – I wanted the part even more badly.

"Wow," I said, which wasn't quite the wise and scholarly response I had been aiming for but it was all that came out.

"Good," Jeremy said, his smile warming as he looked at his watch. "Right – well, we have twenty minutes left, so let's read again."

The second time he told me I was being too large. I took offence initially and said that I was only thirteen and that it wasn't actually healthy to diet at my age. When he pointed out that he was not referring to my size but my acting, I was only a bit less offended.

"Large?" I asked him.

He nodded.

"Yes – look, you've done TV work, haven't you?" I nodded. "Well, imagine your face on a screen that's a thousand times bigger than a TV screen. Every tiny little twitch, every tiny little hair magnified to giant proportions." I thought of the spot that Mum and I had spent several minutes trying to cover up this morning.

"Ew," I said.

"Exactly – well the same goes for your acting. In film you don't need to act large. Keep it small, but precise." He looked at his watch again. "Well, Ruby, our time is up, I'm afraid." I felt a wave of panic well up in my chest.

"But – I haven't done it small yet! Can't we do it quickly being small like you said?" I pleaded, my voice high and stupid again. "I'm too large!"

Jeremy smiled.

"Just remember everything we've talked about and – if you can – I *promise* you that you will do splendidly. Come on, we have to read for Art and Lisa now."

There was something about the way he said Lisa's name that made my stomach contract, because I knew that Lisa didn't like me.

"Are assistant directors' opinions very important?" I asked him in a very small voice. Jeremy gave me a sympathetic look and squeezed my shoulder as we walked to where Art and Lisa would be waiting.

"Let's just say that this one's is," he said.

Something had happened when Jeremy and I acted the scene for Mr Dubrovnik and Lisa Wells, something that had never happened to me before.

For those ten minutes I forgot myself entirely. I forgot I was acting, forgot that I was reading lines, because for those few minutes I was Polly Harris, just discovering the truth about the father she loved. On the brink of understanding that in fact he was an evil historian who had kidnapped her at birth and was planning to sacrifice her at the precise moment the nine planets aligned, in an insane bid to bring about the end of the world. I felt Polly's pain and confusion, her shock and fear, all mixed up with the feelings I had and could still remember from the night that Dad left us. Polly's feelings and my feelings ran together likes two colours of paint mixing until we were one new shade and until I believed in her, I really believed in her. And whatever happened, I knew I had done my very best; I knew I could be proud of myself.

There had been a few moments' silence as Jeremy and I had finished the scene and I saw Art Dubrovnik and Lisa Wells exchange looks.

"Well, thank you, Ruby," Mr Dubrovnik said. "As you probably know our schedule for casting the part of Polly is very tight. We start filming really soon, so we'll make a decision by the end of the day."

I nodded, feeling a little dreamy as the hotel suite came back into focus around me. I was still half in Polly's world.

"OK," I managed to say. I looked at Jeremy. "Thank you for today," I said. "It was amazing to have the chance to meet you and learn from you. Maybe if one day you didn't have anything on you could come and do a masterclass at the academy. I'm sure Ms Lighthouse would love it. We've had a few famous actors – we had Brett Summers last year, who used to play my mum in *Kensington Heights*, although that *was* before the rehab. But I bet you'd be much better than her, all she talked about was herself and her new revised biography."

Jeremy smiled and shook my hand.

"Well, if I happen to find myself one day with 'nothing on', I'll pop by," he said. "And well done – you really listened."

That was an hour ago. I looked at my watch. Anne-Marie had been in there for nearly fifteen minutes longer than I had. They had been so strict about time in my audition, why were they letting hers run over the allocated slot? Perhaps they loved her so much they had offered her the part on the spot and were talking contracts.

I thought about how I would feel if Anne-Marie came out of there with the part already hers. I rehearsed it like

Oscar nominees practise their loser's face just as much as they practise their acceptance speeches. Gracious, happy and excited for her. Dignified. No, not bothered. That's how I would be or at least that's how I would *act*.

Suddenly the door opened and Mr Dubrovnik, Lisa Wells and Jeremy Fort followed a beaming and rosy-cheeked Anne-Marie into the room. With her skin glowing and her eyes sparkling, Anne-Marie looked really lovely, and I thought that that was it; they'd given her the part just because she was so beautiful.

"Ooooh!" A little stifled scream came from over my left shoulder, and I realised it was because Mum had spotted Jeremy Fort, who she fancied in an embarrassingly immature way.

"*Mum!*" I growled at her through my teeth.

"*Janice!*" Dad growled too, simultaneously, and both Mum and I looked sharply at him.

"Sorry. Force of habit," he muttered, and Mum rolled her eyes.

"Well, Sylvia," Art Dubrovnik said, "you certainly have brought me two very fine students today. You can be proud of them – and your academy."

"Of course," Sylvia Lighthouse said, as if she had expected the world's leading film director to compliment her exactly as he had.

"I have two other girls to see after lunch," Mr Dubrovnik told all of us, "and then I'll call Ms Lighthouse at the academy to let you know either way. But I want you to know that you were both great, really great. If you don't get this part it's not because you're not brilliant young actresses."

Anne-Marie and I smiled, and she reached out her fingers and caught my hand and squeezed it.

"Good luck," Mr Dubrovnik said.

And that was it.

It was over.

Chapter Seven

"Action!"

The afternoon felt sort of
like walking through clear
jelly: I could see everything
and hear everything that was going on around me, but I
felt separated from the real world as if I were floating
alongside it rather than being part of it.

We discussed it at length over lunch, all of us –
Anne-Marie, Danny, Nydia and I, and even Menakshi,
Jade and Michael Henderson, about how we might find
out the news.

"If it's bad news," Anne-Marie said, "she'll call us
into her office. She'll give us a speech on taking rejection
on the chin and keeping our chins up. A lot of her
speeches are about chins – have you noticed?"

"But if it's good," Menakshi said, "she might make an
announcement to the whole school in a special
assembly, like when Wade Jackson two years above us
got that record contract." Menakshi looked thoughtful.
"Whatever happened to Wade Jackson?"

"The fickle finger of fame moved on," Danny said,

doing a passable impersonation of Sylvia Lighthouse delivering the catchphrase that seemed to be closest to her heart.

Anne-Marie and I looked at each other.

"But if it's bad news for both of us, it will definitely be in her office," I said.

"What if it's only good news for *one* of you?" Nydia, who had been quiet until that moment, asked me. "What then?"

"She'll call us into her office and tell us together," Anne-Marie said before I could answer. "And there won't be any hard feelings, will there, Ruby? I'll be as happy if Ruby gets the part as if I do."

There were a few muttered "Yeah, rights", groans and giggles at that.

"I will!" Anne-Marie protested.

"Well it might be neither of us," I said simply. "Those other girls they saw this afternoon might be exactly what they were looking for."

I thought about what it would mean to get the part of Polly Harris in *The Lost Treasure of King Arthur* and my insides did a series of complicated Olympic-gold-medal-winning gymnastics. I took a breath and steadied my voice.

"And anyway, if one of us does get it, it means really big changes. Going away from school and home for ages. Getting an on-set tutor! It will all be really different. Maybe it would be better not to get it," I said, feeling suddenly anxious.

Nydia looked at me sharply.

"You don't mean that," she said darkly. I half-smiled.

"I don't suppose I do," I said, "but it is a scary thought!" Normally Nydia would have caught my half-smile and stretched it into a full-sized one as she returned it to me. But this time she didn't smile back at me.

As everyone else filed back to class, I had fallen into step with Nydia, letting Anne-Marie and the others walk ahead.

"Nydia," I said. "You're cross with me."

"I'm not." Nydia was terrible at lying.

"You so are," I said reproachfully. "You didn't call me to wish me good luck like you did Anne-Marie."

Nydia rolled her eyes.

"Because I know that you don't need any luck," she said sharply.

I stopped walking.

"What do you *mean* I don't need any luck?" I asked her. Nydia stopped too and turned round to look at me.

"Well," she said, "you got called back. You got called back when you did the worst audition in the history of the world! Why? Because you are Ruby Parker. I don't think you even had to audition really; I think they would have given you the part whatever. This whole thing was probably just one big publicity stunt for the film."

I stared at her and thought about what Art Dubrovnik had said to me that morning, and my heart sank. *You've got history, Ruby, you've worked in TV.* But then I remembered what else he had said.

"I got called back because Imogene Grant liked my audition," I said. "She said I had something about me that might be right for the part. *That's* why I got called back. Because what the star says goes." Nydia raised an eyebrow.

"So not because you were any good then?" she asked me, turning on her heel and walking off down the corridor.

"Nydia!" I called after her. "I can't believe you are being like this!"

"I was better than you," she said as I caught up with her. "I was better than you, but I didn't get called back because I'm big and ugly and nobody in the world would believe that a big fat girl was Imogene Grant's sister!"

"Nydia, I…" I didn't know what to say. I remembered how I felt when I looked at Anne-Marie, so tall and pretty and blonde, sparkling like a diamond when she came out of the audition. I felt like the ugly duckling then, and I suppose Nydia must have felt the same since the moment she didn't get called back.

"Nydia," I said, "maybe you're right. Maybe it isn't fair. You probably were better than me. And it probably does have something to do with *Kensington Heights*. But – what could I have done about that? Not gone to the audition? Said, 'No thanks very much, I'll pass'?"

Nydia shook her head and looked at her feet, sighing heavily.

"I've got an audition," she said in a quiet voice. "Ms Lighthouse put me forward for it. It's for three episodes of *Holby City*. It's a proper part, with lines and everything. A lot of lines actually."

"Nydia! Your first ever speaking part. I bet you're excited!" I hugged her impulsively, but she didn't hug me back. "That's wonderful," I said, a little less enthusiastically.

"It's for a morbidly obese teenager with early onset diabetes," Nydia said miserably. "That's all I ever get – fat roles, funny roles, idiot roles. I'll never be like you or Anne-Marie."

"Nobody will ever be like Anne-Marie!" I said, trying to make a joke and failing.

As Nydia looked up at me her eyes were shining with tears. "Nothing ever happens to me, Ruby," she said.

"Things always happen to you. I just wish, I just wish that *sometimes* things would happen to me." I picked up her hands.

"I bet you get this part in *Holby City*," I said.

"Maybe," she said. "But I don't want *that* part! I want to be an action hero, a romantic lead. But no, I'm stuck inside this stupid fat ugly body and I can't get out! And I'm jealous of you. I'm jealous and angry that no matter how good I am, even when I'm better than you I'll never beat you. I'll never get a part we both go for. Unless it's the part of a fat ugly person."

We stood, both of us, in the empty corridor, the bell calling us to class ringing in our ears.

"I don't know what to say," I said at last as the chimes died away and we were both officially late. "I didn't know how unhappy you were. I thought you were happy with how you looked. Always joking about it."

"Before anybody else does," Nydia said.

"Well, Nydia, if you are unhappy then things don't have to stay the same, they can change – you can change. And I'll help you."

"How will you help me?" Nydia asked me.

"Well, you could talk to the school nurse for starters. Ask her about a healthy-eating plan. And maybe she could talk to your mum for you."

"Mum will kill me if she thinks I've been talking about her cooking to anyone," Nydia said.

"But does your mum know how unhappy you are?" I asked. She shook her head. "I think your mum would kill you if she knew that you had been hiding it from her."

"You must think I'm a greedy fat pig," Nydia said quietly.

"Nydia!" I said. "Of course I don't. I think that you and me eat almost the same thing every day, and I'm not a stick insect. And actually, I think you are beautiful just as you are. But if you're this unhappy, it's worth finding out about, right? I'll come with you, if you like, to see the nurse." Finally, Nydia gave me a half-smile.

"Really?" she said.

"Of course," I said.

"What – even if you're off shooting your first movie?"

"Even if," I said, and then I laughed. "Not that I'm going to get that part in a million years. Anne-Marie is miles prettier than me."

"I'm sorry I got jealous," Nydia said.

"I'm sorry," I said. "I got so caught up in all of this I wasn't a very good friend. Anne-Marie says friendship comes second when you're an actor, but I don't think so. I think that no matter what happens, friendship should always come first."

When we got to class it didn't matter that we were late. The entire class was out of their desks and gathered around two large windows, including Mr Barlow the maths teacher.

"Sorry we're— What's going on?" Nydia asked, and Mr Barlow turned round.

"There you are, Ruby!" he exclaimed. "Come and see! I think that the field has just narrowed rather considerably. I don't suppose they came out here to issue rejections."

I rushed to the window and elbowed my way past Menakshi to Anne-Marie's side. Just pulling up to the main entrance of the school was a red convertible Rolls Royce carrying two passengers – Art Dubrovnik and Lisa Wells.

"It's one of us," Anne-Marie said, her voice as high and as taught as a tightrope. Her hand darted out and gripped my wrist hard.

"Ouch," I said.

"Sorry," Anne-Marie said, but she didn't let go.

"It might not be one of us," I started cautiously. "Maybe they were just in the area and—"

"Oh, shut up, idiot," Anne-Marie said. So I did.

We watched as the pair walked up the steps to the

entrance, greeted halfway by Ms Lighthouse. They spoke for a few moments and then Ms Lighthouse nodded emphatically and led them inside.

It seemed like years before we heard Mrs Moore's footsteps in the corridor. She knocked on the open door and waited for Mr Barlow to invite her in before she entered.

"I'm sorry to interrupt you, Mr Barlow," Mrs Moore said. Mrs Moore was always terribly polite, which was usually quite funny, but right at that moment seemed like a dreadful waste of time.

"Nothing much to interrupt here at the moment, Mrs Moore," Mr Barlow said cheerfully. He nodded at Anne-Marie and me. "I think we'll have to put these two out of their misery before I get this lot back to equations. I take it you want to take Ruby and Anne-Marie out of class?"

Mrs Moore nodded. "Yes, please, Mr Barlow. Thank you very much." She glanced at the two of us impassively. "Come along, girls," she said. And clutching each other's hands, Anne-Marie and I followed her.

"Hey, girls," Nydia called out. I turned and looked at her. "Break a leg," she said with a smile. But I was almost certain it was an actor's smile – a fake one.

Mr Dubrovnik and Lisa Wells were sitting opposite Ms Lighthouse's desk when we came in, drinking tea out of Ms Lighthouse's flowery china cups. Art Dubrovnik smiled at us, and Lisa Wells looked us up and down with an air of decided disappointment.

"Take a seat, girls," Ms Lighthouse said. We saw that two classroom chairs had been brought in for us to sit on, so we sat down. Every second ticked by as if an hour had been inserted in between.

"Well," Sylvia Lighthouse said, leaning forward on her desk and pressing her fingers together. "I am delighted that Mr Dubrovnik and... his associate have come out to see us today. Delighted because as I am sure you have worked out by now it means that one of you two girls has got the part of Polly Harris. And I am proud but not surprised to hear that both of you were excellent, beating all the other candidates hands down. We thought it would be a good idea for Mr Dubrovnik and Ms Wells to talk to you together so that you can both hear from the horse's mouth, as it were, exactly how proud you can be of what you have achieved." Sylvia gestured to Art Dubrovnik that she was handing the conversation over to him. I glanced at Anne-Marie and wondered if she was thinking the same thing that I was which was mainly: JUST TELL US NOW!

"Ruby, Anne-Marie," Art said. "I've got to tell you

that you were both wonderful today. You both brought different qualities to the reading, you each played the role differently but brilliantly, and in the end we weren't deciding on who was the better actor but on whose interpretation of Polly Harris most fitted the film." Art Dubrovnik paused – one of the long excruciating pauses that are scripted on TV talent shows to keep viewers hooked and contestants guessing, but which in real life, my life especially, are just plain cruel.

"In the end," Mr Dubrovnik pulled down the corners of his mouth in a kind of upside-down smile, "I didn't make the final decision. I let my leading lady make the final choice because I knew it was vital that she picked the girl she would most get on with and who fitted her vision of Flame and Ember's relationship.

"Imogene Grant?" Anne-Marie said, quickly looking out of the window to where the Rolls Royce was still parked, empty except for the chauffeur. "But how did she choose? On the Internet or a webcam or something?"

I stared at Anne-Marie. I didn't care if Imogene Grant saw us through a trans-global crystal ball, I just wanted to know WHO HAD THE PART. But nobody else seemed to notice that.

"No," Art Dubrovnik said, smiling. "Actually, she saw your audition in the flesh. Both times." Mr Dubrovnik looked at Lisa Wells.

"Imogene – do you want to tell them yourself?" Lisa Wells nodded and Anne-Marie and I looked at each other, confused.

Lisa Wells took off her thick black glasses and set them on Ms Lighthouse's desk. And then slowly and incredibly she peeled *off* her long sharp pointy nose to reveal a much prettier and very familiar one underneath. She followed that by removing with some difficulty the thick orange eyebrows one by one, wincing as if she were removing a very sticky plaster. Then, cupping her hand under each eye, she pinched out the fishy blue contact lenses, and when she'd blinked a few times you could see they were now a soft amber-brown colour.

Anne-Marie and I watched all of this open-mouthed until finally the wiry orange wig was removed and the woman underneath it shook out her long soft honey-brown curls and smiled at us. She smiled the million-dollar smile. She smiled Imogene Grant's smile. And finally I realised that, with all the tension, I hadn't started seeing things; finally I realised that Lisa Wells *was* Imogene Grant. She had been all along.

"Wow!" Anne-Marie spoke first. "That is *amazing*, you are such an *amazing* actress. I had no idea... *Wow!*"

"You saw me throw up!" I said before my brain could stop my tongue from moving.

Imogene Grant laughed and lit up the room. She was the most beautiful woman I had ever seen. Even more lovely in real life than when she was airbrushed to perfection on a magazine cover or lit in soft focus for a film. She was even more beautiful because she was real: really, *really* real.

"But, I mean," Anne-Marie said, "I've seen all your films and I read every article about you I can find, and there you were all along and I didn't notice you. You completely transformed yourself!"

I noticed that Anne-Marie was managing all the compliments while all I had done was remind her about the whole vomiting thing. I tried to make up for it.

"Really great false nose," I said. Imogene laughed again - at least she thought I was funny.

"Thanks," she said. "I borrowed it from Nicole. But look, the real reason you didn't spot it was me wasn't because of the disguise; it was because when I had this wig on I became Lisa Wells – or at least my version of her. I *was* her, so there was no Imogene Grant for you to notice."

"You are an amazing actress," Anne-Marie said.

"You really are," I said, determined not to be left out when it came to showering compliments. Imogene beamed at us.

"I'm sorry to shock you, girls. I wanted to be in the

auditions but I was afraid of throwing the candidates off. I have to dress up in disguises a lot just to get around town, you know, on the bus or whatever, without people mobbing me."

Anne-Marie and I looked amazed at each other. Imogene Grant on the bus?

"I think you put me off more as Lisa Wells than you would have as Imogene Grant," I said. Imogene nodded.

"Well that was a little test Art and I came up with between ourselves. We needed the person who plays Polly Harris's character to have guts and determination, to carry on no matter what happens. And you both did!" She smiled at us again. "So I hope that you both forgive me. I hope I wasn't too scary."

"You were *wonderful*," Anne-Marie said sincerely. "An amazing performance."

I looked at Ms Lighthouse to see if she was as shocked as we were and saw that she was perfectly serene. She had known all along. I started to feel annoyed. I mean I was thrilled and excited that I had just met Imogene Grant, and proud and happy that I had auditioned for Art Dubrovnik and acted with Jeremy Fort. I was practically delirious! But at that point there was really only one thing that I wanted to know.

"Who got the part?" I asked Imogene Grant straight

out. "I'm sorry, I don't mean to be rude; you are completely my hero and I know I should just shut up and wait, but please – before I explode or implode or *something* – can you just tell us? Who got the part?"

Imogene Grant smiled at me and glanced at Mr Dubrovnik.

"*You* got the part, Ruby," she said. "In the end we wanted your vulnerability, your sense of humour in the role." I let her words wash over me and then slowly, slowly sink in. I glanced at Anne-Marie who had her Oscar nominee loser's smile perfectly placed on her lovely face.

"Anne-Marie," Imogene turned to her. "We loved your feisty, funny portrayal of the character, and I can see you have a great talent, but in this one case it wasn't what we needed for the film. But please don't give up. Your time will come, I am certain of that. I'll keep you in mind for any future projects I have."

Anne-Marie nodded and her smile seemed a little more real this time. She hooked her arm around my neck and kissed me on the cheek.

"You did it, Ruby," she said, jiggling me up and down as she hugged me. "You did it!"

And finally I realised exactly what I had done.

I had got the part. And now? Now everything would change.

teen girl! Magazine's Girly Gossip Weekly

all YOU need to know to be in the know!

And this week Girly Gossip has got plenty of showbiz gossip and rumours to tantalise you with.

We can exclusively reveal that Justin de Souza is single again after a stormy relationship with girl-band dropout Sandy Sanderson.

So keep on your toes, girls, Justin's available – again…

Also fresh from the *Kensington Heights* set rumours are running high that new face Danny Harvey is starting to get more fan mail than Justin and is overtaking him as most popular teen.

Who would you prefer? Blond clean-cut Justin or dark brooding Danny? Girly Gossip knows who we prefer and let's just say he hasn't recently been dumped by a rubbish pop star!

Still, we'll have to put those dreams on hold because Danny is still dating ex-*Kensington Heights* star Ruby Parker…

Talking of our old friend Ruby, we've got some very exciting news. If the rumours are true then it looks like our very own home-grown talent, Ruby Parker, has been cast in next year's biggest summer blockbuster, *The Lost Treasure of King Arthur*. Girly Gossip favourite Ruby will be acting alongside legends of the big screen Imogene Grant, your mum's faves Jeremy Fort and Harry McLean and… wait for it… Sean Rivers! Swoon!

Good luck, Ruby, and let us know what Sean Rivers is really like, won't you? **Girly Gossip** just loves him!

"Action!"

Chapter Eight

I sat up in bed, wide awake in the dark, and I knew I had to be somewhere, I just couldn't remember exactly where. As I tried to get out of bed I thumped my head against the cold, hard painted surface of a wall that was somehow on the wrong side of my bed. I sank back in bed and rubbed my forehead. It was still dark in the room and it took a few half-asleep moments for me to work out where I was.

"The flat," I grumbled to myself. The flat Mum and I were renting in Watford during shooting so that I could get to the set at Elm Tree Studios on time without having to get up before dawn. We had moved in just last night and I hadn't got used to it yet, including the position of the bed in an unfamiliar room.

Tentatively I dangled my toes over the other side of the bed until they reached the soft pile carpet. I rubbed my eyes and waited for them to adjust to the gloom. Eventually I could see a thin sliver of light under the bedroom door. Mum was already up, probably making me a good breakfast even though she knew I would be too nervous to eat it. How could I ever eat anything when it was my first day on set?

My first day on set. On a film set. I kept saying the words over and over again in my mind, but it still didn't seem real. In fact, nothing had seemed especially real since that afternoon in Ms Lighthouse's office when I found out I had got the part.

First there had been the congratulations.

When I left that day the whole school had cheered me off, clapping and whistling as I went. Everybody was acting as if they'd been my best friends for years. Menakshi had grabbed me, hugged and kissed me. Jade had told me she *knew* I was going to get the part and she couldn't think who deserved it more. And gradually, as I had collected all my things, word spread from class to class and people came out into the corridor and followed me as I made my way out of the building. Everyone followed me clapping and cheering, including Danny, holding my hand. All of them – everyone – acting as if they were my best and oldest friends. All of them, that is, except for my actual best and oldest friend, Nydia, who followed the parade but hardly looked at me, let alone said anything nice.

As we reached the front entrance of the academy I saw that Art Dubrovnik and Imogene Grant were waiting in the Rolls Royce.

"We thought we'd give you a lift home," Mr Dubrovnik said.

"Wow!" I said. Danny hugged me tightly and kissed me briefly on the mouth.

"I'm so proud of you, Ruby," he said, smiling. "Call me later, yeah?" I nodded and turned to Nydia.

"I meant what I said," I told her, leaning closer to her so that she could hear me.

"I know you did," she said, but her voice was stiff. She smiled briefly and squeezed my hand. "You'll be great, Ruby, you always are."

And as Mr Dubrovnik and Imogene Grant took me home in the red Rolls Royce to break the news to my mum, maybe all of the school was out waving and cheering as we drove off.

"They love you," Imogene Grant said, smiling at me.

"No, it must be you," I said. "Big film star."

"Can't be me," she said, laughing, and as I looked at her I noticed she had her orange wig and glasses on again.

"I'm just Lisa Wells," she said, and we laughed together.

Me and Imogene Grant laughing in the back of a red Rolls Royce convertible. Now if that's not unreal I don't know what is.

When Mum found out there was crying and gushing and smiling, and picking up pairs of discarded shoes and chucking them hurriedly in cupboards as she showed an A-list film star and director into her living room as if those kind of people dropped round at least three times a week. When Dad arrived a few minutes later he wasn't much better. He kept picking me up and hugging me, ruffling my hair so much I thought I'd end up having to wear the wig. And he kept staring at Imogene Grant, I mean literally gawping at her. Which was fair, I supposed, as Mum had done the same thing to Jeremy Fort earlier that day, but it was still embarrassing. The adults talked and talked about how things would work out while I just sat and let it all go on above my head. I was still in shock.

Then there was the money.

Mum and Dad had agreed my *Kensington Heights* contracts in the past, but with this, Sylvia Lighthouse herself got involved because she really understood the complexities of the contract. So the next day after school Mum, Dad and I had a meeting in her office to talk about the money with Audrey Goldman my agent. She was sort of everybody's agent really, and worked for more or less the whole school at one time or another because Sylvia said she was the best. She checked the contracts and negotiated the fees. I didn't really see her much, though, because up until that moment my *Kensington Heights* contracts had always been more or less the same, so Mum talked to her about them over the phone. I had never been allowed to listen in on the money bits before so I was really excited to know how much I was getting.

I was glad we had Audrey Gold because when they started to talk about the contract I understood about one word in two hundred. So I waited and waited and waited for them to talk about the one thing I was fascinated by – how much money was a lot of money. I mean of *course* I cared more about the actual opportunity than the money, and yes, I *would* have done it for nothing at all. But for all the years I was working on *Kensington Heights* all I got was an allowance every week, and that was less than some kids at school who didn't work on a prime-time soap. And all because Mum wanted me to have a normal childhood and learn solid values, like not having the best mobile phone until it's been out for a year and comes free with a pay-as-you-go tariff and by then everyone else has got a better one anyway. That sort of thing. And I had learned them, I thought. Nobody was more normal than me. And anyway, this was the first time I had ever been to a money meeting, so I waited through all the gobbledygook until they finally said what I had been waiting to hear.

"Two hundred thousand pounds," Audrey Gold said. "How does that sound?"

"Blimey," I said, and all three adults looked at me as if they had forgotten I was there.

"To go into your trust," my mum said promptly, looking at Dad who nodded.

"Mum!" I protested. "Dad!"

"Well, maybe you can have a little bit," she said. "Buy some new things and perhaps have a little wrap party for all your friends. We could redecorate your bedroom if you like? I know you think it's too babyish."

"Only because I've had that fairy wallpaper since I was six," I said, trying to remember not to bring up an old argument. "Or," I added casually, "we could always have a swimming pool."

"We'd never fit one in the garden," Mum said.

"We could buy a house with one built in?" I suggested. Mum smiled at me like I was next-door's toddler saying something sweet and funny and said, "Two hundred thousand pounds isn't enough to buy a house like that in London, dear." And I felt sort of deflated. I still didn't know exactly how much was waiting for me to turn twenty-one in my trust fund. And as far as I was concerned two hundred thousand pounds made me rich beyond my wildest dreams. Except that it turned out that that much money actually made me rich just a little bit short of one of my more tame dreams. A house with a swimming pool was way down on my list, after a private jet and my own paradise island.

"Is it right, that amount?" my dad asked. "Is it worth negotiating?" Audrey Gold drew her mouth into a thin line and shrugged. "Well, Ruby has almost zero profile over the pond, unless you count *Kensington Heights* running on BBC America, but I'd say given that they start shooting in ten days it's worth a shot."

And there were a lot of phone calls and lots of conversations and a lot of Mum and Dad spending time together talking about me, without arguing or falling out, and after a couple of days my mum came up to my bedroom and said, "We're ready to sign, Ruby, but before we do, are you sure you want to do this? To be taken out of school and work really hard on this film? Your whole life will completely change because of this. Things might never be the same as they are now."

I stared at her.

"Are you bonkers?" I said. "Of course I want to do it!"

"Just checking," she said. And as she went back down the stairs she was singing. I hadn't heard her singing in ages.

Finally there were the goodbyes.

Mum and Dad took Nydia, Anne-Marie, Danny and me to our favourite pizza restaurant. And I thought that had to mean something because before they split up we used to come here at least twice a month. It was one of our special places. Since Dad had moved out and until I got that second audition for the film, we hadn't been anywhere together. And now I was sure that Dad saw more of Mum than he did of his so-called "girlfriend". I smiled at them happily. "This is great, isn't it? Being all together." Mum and Dad swapped looks across the table.

"Yes, love," Mum said with a small smile.

"Great," Dad said, looking carefully at his menu. It seemed as if although they didn't mind spending time together, they didn't actually want to talk about it.

"Good evening, everyone," Cassie said as she came to take our order. "Hi, Ruby, I really miss you in *Kensington Heights*, but I have to say I love *your* character, Danny – Marcus is brilliant. Actually, I'll have to get you to sign something before you go because my little sister loves you!"

"No problem," Danny said, looking a little embarrassed as he glanced at me.

"Danny's very popular with little girls," Anne-Marie said mischievously, winking at me over the top of her glass.

"Oh, don't let Suzie hear you say that!" Cassie said with a laugh. "She's nearly fourteen! All of her pals think you are the bee's knees, Danny." I watched a blush spread across Danny's cheeks and tried not to feel jealous of some girl I had never met and who Danny would probably never meet. "I expect you'll be the next one to move on to bigger things," Cassie added.

Danny shrugged.

"Oh, I don't know," he said. "I think kids our age only get these chances once in a blue moon."

"Or if there's a *Harry Potter* film being shot," Anne-Marie pointed out. "And there's always a *Harry Potter* film being shot; it's as regular as Christmas for kid actors. Should hopefully see a good few of us through to adulthood. Although not me," she finished with a little twist of her mouth. "I don't care though, cos Art Dubrovnik's considering me for his next project, isn't he, Ruby?"

"He is," I said, even though I didn't think that was exactly what he had said.

Cassie smiled at all of us, her pen hovering above her pad.

"So are we ready to order?" she asked brightly.

We were halfway through our pizzas when I noticed that Nydia had hardly touched hers. Instead, she picked at her side salad without much enthusiasm. I remembered the conversation we'd had in the school corridor with the bell clanging in our ears.

"Are you OK?" I said, keeping my voice low.

"Fine," she said quite loudly, smiling at me.

"I've thought about it and I know I won't be around for a while, but I'll get days off and I'll come back and then on one of those days we could go and see the nurse..."

"No, it's fine," Nydia said. "Honestly. I don't need to see the nurse and make a big fuss. I'm fine now."

"But I—"

"Really," Nydia said, picking up a slice of pizza and biting the end off it. She spoke through her mouthful. "I was just being silly and jealous and overdramatic. I'm fine now, really. There's no problem, honestly." I looked carefully at Nydia's face to see if she was keeping something from me. Normally I could tell straight away because Nydia's lying skills are absolutely appalling. But this time I wasn't sure. She held my look with her chin tipped up a little, and I realised that even if things weren't "fine" with her at the moment then, *right now,* at least, she didn't need or want my help.

"Well, if you change your mind," I said.

"OK," Nydia said and smiled that funny new smile of hers that seemed almost upside-down.

"Nydia, is there something—?" I started to ask her.

"I still can't believe," Anne-Marie said, cutting through our conversation, "that you are going to meet *THE Sean Rivers,* that you are going to act with *THE Sean Rivers.* Ooh, ooh!" She flapped her hands like a frantic starling. "You might even have a kissing scene! Oh my gosh, I'd do anything to have a kissing scene with *THE Sean Rivers!*" She gave me a sly little smile and raised an eyebrow. "Actually, as I'm second favourite for the role and shooting starts in two days, if I just pushed you down the stairs to the ladies…" She giggled and everyone else laughed including me, even though I knew that there was at least five per cent of Anne-Marie that hadn't been joking. I just hoped that the remaining ninety-five per cent of her was more than enough to stop her actually going through with it.

After dinner Mum and Dad dropped Nydia and Anne-Marie off and Danny said he'd walk from our house as it wasn't far. I swear Mum and Dad hung around for at least twenty seconds, waiting for me to go inside with them, before they got the hint and realised I wanted to say goodbye to Danny on my own.

Alone at last, I walked Danny to the gate and we stood under the orange glow of the streetlight.

"I'm going to miss you," Danny said, looking at his trainers. "And stuff."

"And me," I said, tucking my hand into the pocket of his jacket. "But I'm only going to Watford. And Mum says when I have days off she'll bring me back to visit. We'll have to come back anyway to make sure that next door are only feeding Everest the amount he's supposed to have and not the amount he wants. Otherwise, when we come back for good we won't be able to get in the house – it will be full of fat cat!" Danny smiled and looked into my eyes. I held my breath.

"You look seriously orange under this streetlamp," he said.

"Oh, the romance!" I said, laughing. Danny smiled.

"Look, Ruby, you know, don't you, that those fan letters are nice and everything. But they don't mean anything to me. I don't care who fancies me except you, no matter what *Teen Girl! Magazine* thinks."

"I know," I said, feeling stupid for being jealous of Cassie's little sister and anyone else like her out there who fancied *my* boyfriend. "I'm so over that."

"Did you see that bit in *Teen Girl!* about you being cast in the film?" he asked me. I nodded; it was hard to miss it. Mum had cut it out, blown it up to poster size and stuck it on the wall. "Because – well, you're not going to want to go out with this Sean Rivers bloke, are you?" he said sort of quickly and under his breath. I laughed.

"Sean Rivers wouldn't look twice at me!" I told him.

"I bet he would," Danny said. "But that's not what I asked. I asked you if you fancied him?" I shook my head and then lied it almost right off my shoulders.

"Not even a bit," I said. Luckily I was a slightly better liar than Nydia.

"Good," Danny said. "Cos I'll miss you, Rube. Loads."

He kissed me then under the streetlamp and for the first time I wondered if I really wanted to go and be a movie star after all, because even though I wanted some things to change, other things – Danny things – I wanted to stay exactly the same.

"Bye then," I said, as he took a step back and gazed at me intently.

"You look so..." he started shyly.

"Yes?" I said breathlessly.

"...Orange!" he said, laughing. "It's like you've eaten about two tons of carrots!"

"Danny!" I said, laughing too. He smiled at me and blew me a kiss.

"You know I think you're the prettiest girl in world," he said, as he began to walk backwards. "Text me when you get there, phone me as soon as you can and tell me everything, and let me know when you're coming back for your days off, OK?"

"OK," I said, and stood and watched him turn his back and get smaller and smaller under each pool of streetlight until I couldn't see him any more.

I still couldn't believe that I, Ruby Parker, had a boyfriend like Danny Harvey. So what if I'd had a crush on Sean Rivers since I was twelve? I promised myself when I finally met him I'd be nothing but professionally friendly. I wouldn't even notice his incredible good looks.

Because no one, not even Sean Rivers, could ever be as good a boyfriend as Danny Harvey.

That last night before we left for Watford I felt like the luckiest girl in the world. But as I sat on the edge of a strange bed in a strange flat about to do something I hardly dared to dream of, I felt petrified.

Mum pushed open my bedroom door and the light from the hallway flooded in.

"I've brought you some tea," she said, setting it down beside the strange bed. "How are you feeling?"

"Fine," I said. "A bit sick actually."

"Well, you'll be fine with a good breakfast inside you," Mum said. "There's bacon and eggs waiting for you in the kitchen." She smiled at me. "This is it, Ruby! Today's the first day of you being a movie star. This is the day when everything changes."

I swallowed and nodded and got back into bed and pulled the duvet right over my head.

Chapter Nine

Sometimes when I was working on *Kensington Heights* I'd get picked up in a car from home if I had a very early shoot, or dropped off in one after a late finish. I used to feel really important getting picked up in a people carrier or a four-wheel drive.

But when Mum and I opened the front door to the apartment block we were staying in and saw an actual stretch limo waiting to take us to the studio, we couldn't believe it.

"I feel underdressed," my mum said, running her fingers through her hair, which was a lie anyway as she was as dressed up and with as much make-up on as when she went out on one of her nights. More dressed up, actually, because she had high-heeled, peep-toed sandals on. In *November*! And she never usually wore heels. I didn't know why she had made such an effort. I mean all she would be doing all day was hanging around in make-up, hanging around on set, or maybe hanging around in our Winnebago.

Winnebago! I smiled with delight at the almost magic word as we slid into the back of the limousine. It was a lot like stepping into the Tardis, I'd imagine. It was huge inside. Really long, the floor and ceiling lit with ropes of sparkling lights. There was a TV set in one corner and what might have been a fridge. Mum and I sat stiffly on the back seat and looked around us. I think both of us were afraid to move or touch anything.

"Goodness me," Mum said, laughing nervously. "A limo to pick you up and a Winnebago. Whatever next?"

I thought about what our Winnebago would be like. It was really just a very big, very posh caravan that actors could rest in, eat in, or read their lines in while they were not required on set. And the Winnebago was a sort of currency among film actors, because the bigger the Winnebago, the bigger the star.

It was a bit like the size of the star you had stuck on your dressing-room door in TV or the theatre. (The star on my ex-TV mum Brett Summers's door had been the biggest one I had ever seen, but I found out just before I left the show that actually she had made it herself out of the back of a cornflakes packet and glued it on with eyelash glue because the BBC one wasn't big enough. But I wasn't surprised to find out it was false. It turned out that nearly everything about her was false, and all the time I had trusted her and thought of her almost like a real mother, she had been plotting to get me fired from the show because she said I stole every scene we were in together!)

So, the bigger the star, the bigger the Winnebago. I expected Imogene Grant's to be super-sized. Maybe even a two-storey one, with a gym and a Jacuzzi. Jeremy Fort and Harry McLean's would be about the same I guessed. A fully equipped kitchen and king-size bedroom at least. I wasn't sure about Sean Rivers because although he was very famous, he was quite young at just fifteen, and I wasn't sure if being young outweighed being really famous. As I was even younger and not very famous at all, I didn't have too high expectations for mine. But I didn't care. I didn't care if my Winnebago was more like the kind of caravan you might find on a disused campsite in Bridlington. It would be a Winnebago on a film set and it would be *mine*.

Remembering that Danny wanted me to tell him everything, I texted him. "In a limo on way to set and Winnebago!! Rxxx." I held the phone in my hand for a couple of minutes expecting it to fizz and beep in my palm, but it lay dormant. Mum glanced at me.

"He's still in bed I expect, love," she said annoyingly, knowing exactly what I had been doing. "It's not even seven yet."

The studios themselves were not as glamorous as I expected them to be. I suppose I'd thought they'd be shooting loads of different films all at once and that the lot would be crowded with hordes of extras: a legion of Roman soldiers, a gaggle of Victorian cockneys and some dancing cheerleaders. But instead, as the limo pulled through the security gate, the studio seemed largely deserted.

It was much, much bigger than I had imagined. In fact, it wasn't like I had imagined at all. I could see two huge, nearly featureless buildings like aircraft hangars or warehouses side by side, grey with a big orange stripe about two-thirds of the way down. The only distinguishing feature was that the one on the left had a large green number one on it and the one on the right had a number two. I was going to the building marked two. Somewhere else there would be two other identical buildings marked three and four.

It would be inside building two that I would shoot my first scene in *The Lost Treasure of King Arthur*. It wasn't the first scene that Polly appeared in in the story, in fact, it was quite near the end, after she had discovered that she was really Ember Buchanen and was trying to escape Professor Darkly. The scene I was shooting today was where Polly was trapped in the Caverns of Mordred hidden beneath the British Museum, stranded on a tiny ledge above a lethal drop trying to reach out to Flame and Gareth (played by Harry McLean), who were just out of reach on a wider ledge above. I was excited about it, but I hoped that the ledge wouldn't really be too high. I wasn't that keen on heights.

I didn't mind shooting out of sequence; I was used to it. We did it all the time in *Kensington Heights*. Shot all the scenes that took place in one set at once, no matter where they came in the episode. On this film it was done in order of how long it would take to add special effects. The bigger the effects, the earlier the scene was shot. It also depended on the actors. It cost less money to shoot the scenes with all or most of the principal actors in first so that you didn't keep expensive stars hanging around for weeks waiting for their next scene. Polly and Professor Darkly were mostly in the film from the middle to the end. When those scenes were completed, Jeremy Fort and I would be finished until post-production and the other actors would shoot the first half.

I was a bit worried about my first scene being one so far into the film though. I was still feeling like I was getting to know Polly/Ember. I was worried that in this first filmed scene I might get it all wrong, and then when I went back and acted the earlier scenes Polly would seem like a completely different girl. But Art Dubrovnik told me I didn't have to worry. He told me that he had a vision for the whole of the film; he knew exactly how every scene should be. And that if I followed his direction I would be perfect.

The limo drew to a stop outside the hangar and a door opened in the side. A tall young woman holding a clipboard came out and opened the limousine door. She had a belt on with a walkie-talkie attached to it and one of those headsets that hook over your ear with a mouthpiece that comes around the side. She was extremely pretty with big black eyes and a friendly smile. She had the longest hair I've ever seen swinging in tiny beaded plaits right down past her bum.

"You must be Ruby," she said, taking my hand and then surprising me with a kiss on each cheek. "And Ruby's mum, Mrs Parker – Janice, isn't it?" She kissed Mum, who rather awkwardly kissed her back. "Pleased to meet you, I'm Lisa Wells."

"But...?" Mum and I looked at each other and the woman laughed so that the beads in her hair rattled like rain against a window pane.

"The real Lisa Wells." She looked at my nervous face. "Don't worry," she said. "I'm nothing like Imogene's version. That version was mean, wasn't she? I think

Imogene must have had a few tough auditions when she was starting out!"

Lisa showed us into a long, brightly-lit corridor and led us up some stairs, talking all the time as we followed her.

"First stop, we drop in on Art. He'll give you his pep talk and then tell you to call him Art. Second stop, make-up. They'll be making you look sweaty and dirty with a few cuts and bruises, so nice and glamorous! Third stop, wardrobe, run by our 'charming' wardrobe mistress Tallulah Banks. Don't get on the wrong side of her – that woman can hold a grudge." Lisa threw me a grimace over one shoulder. "She's still holding one against me. Don't ask, it's a long story... Anyway," she continued, "you actually appear to wear the same outfit for almost all of the film. But we have thirty-two identical versions each numbered and cross-referenced to where you are in the story. Number one is the neat clean one. Number thirty-two is near the end when you're sinking into a pool of molten lava. You'll be wearing twenty-eight today. It's pretty messed up." She flashed me a smile over her shoulder. "You have three scenes scheduled today."

"Is that all?" I said, surprised. Three scenes in *Kensington Heights* took about an hour. This was a whole day's work and the scenes were much shorter.

"That's right, honey. There's an awful lot of takes before we get the right one. You'll see," Lisa said. She stopped so suddenly that I almost walked into her click-clacking beads. She opened the door of a meeting room.

Sitting around three tables pushed together were Art Dubrovnik, Imogene Grant, Harry McLean and Jeremy Fort. They had their scripts open and Jeremy was making notes in his.

"Ooooh," I heard Mum squeak behind me. I shot her a look and she clamped her mouth shut, trying not to go all gooey at the sight of Jeremy Fort, who was – the last time I looked – going out with a Russian supermodel half Mum's age and width, and so wasn't very likely to fancy her even if she wasn't my mum. I was glad though that Sean Rivers wasn't sitting at the table. If Sean Rivers had been there I would have been dead of heart failure about five seconds later and Anne-Marie would have got her wish after all. I still hadn't worked out how I was going to manage when I actually met him. I might be all right if he stood still and didn't speak or move, but if he smiled at me, that gorgeous, lovely smile from the very end of The Underdogs, then that would be it: the whole heart-failure thing would kick in and my career would be over. I thought about Danny and felt a pang of guilt. Here I was in a room full of some of the world's most famous people and I was going slushy over Sean Rivers (who wasn't even here) when I had a great boyfriend already. I pushed Sean to the back of my mind and made myself focus on Mr Dubrovnik.

"Ruby!" Art Dubrovnik said, standing up and smiling that smile that pushed his whole face upwards. "Come, come – come and sit down. There's coffee and fruit and croissants. Can I get you anything?" I shook my head but he poured Mum and I black coffees anyway and set an orange down next to our cups, as we took the two seats closest to the door.

"You need a good breakfast, right, Mrs Parker?" he said, grinning at my mum.

"I always say so," Mum said, adding, "Call me Janice, please."

"Janice, thank you, I will. Ruby, I've got us all together here this morning because I want you and everyone here to know: you're on a team now. Team *King Arthur*. And on my team *no one* is more important than anyone else. Except me of course," Art chuckled and everyone smiled except Mum who laughed, maybe a little too loudly.

"Now, Ruby," he continued, "you're a very lucky girl. You have three great actors to learn from – four if you count Sean, who is very promising. Learn from them, pay them respect, but don't be afraid of them. They are your colleagues. Your friends. OK?" I nodded and caught Imogene winking at me, which made me feel a bit less nervous.

"OK, Mr Dubrovnik," I said.

"Call me Art, OK?" He grinned at me.

"OK, A... Art," I said, somehow managing to stumble over the short and simple name. "Um," I felt the question forming in my mouth almost before I knew what it was going to be. "Where *is* Sean Rivers?" I asked Art Dubrovnik in a silly high voice, like a lovesick little fan. "Will I get to meet him today?"

Art chuckled and I felt my cheeks grow hot.

"He's not arriving until next week, Ruby; in the scenes you are shooting this week Sean's character, Catcher, is somewhere else in the Caverns of Mordred getting slowly crushed to death in a stone prison with shrinking walls." Art smiled at me. "Don't worry, Ruby, you'll meet him soon enough. Just try not to fall for him, OK? We don't have time for on-set romances – right, Imogene?" Art grinned at Imogene as I considered what my chances of survival would be if I threw myself out of the window. The last thing I wanted Art to think was that I was so unprofessional that I would have a crush on one of my fellow actors. I mean, I might have, but I didn't want *him* to know that!

"Oh, leave Ruby alone, Art," Imogene said mildly, sipping her coffee. Somehow the tone of her voice took some of the heat out of my cheeks. "All Ruby was doing was asking about a fellow actor who is pretty key to her role in the film. I think it's you who'll need some direction here from me – on how to treat teenage girls. Rule number one is don't tease them. Rule number two is DO NOT TEASE THEM. Got it?" Imogene smiled sweetly at Art who gave her a little bow.

"Got it," Art said. "Sorry for teasing you, Miss Parker."

"Were you teasing me?" I asked him, managing to get my own back. "I hadn't noticed."

Art smiled at me.

"You're pretty funny, Ruby," he said. "I like you."

"Art," the real Lisa Wells interrupted us, "we've only got three hours to get this lot through make-up and costume. And we've got the Legions of Mordred downstairs waiting to get zombied up."

"Well, I can see my boss wants you guys," Art said jovially, "so off you go. I'll come round while you're in make-up and talk through the scene with you and then I'll see you all on set."

And that was how it began. That was how my movie career began.

And nothing on the first day went exactly how I had imagined.

I had been in make-up for nearly an hour by the time Art came to see me. In fact, I was almost asleep because Natasha the make-up lady told me I had to close my eyes while she applied a deep bloody gash to my temple, which seemed to take for ever.

"Ruby," Art said, making me jump a little in my chair, which made Natasha hiss through her teeth.

"Hello, Mr Dubrovnik, Art, I mean," I said, opening one eye and looking sideways at him." Natasha clamped a hand on my head and repositioned it with a huff. Natasha was quite scary.

"Don't move," she told me. "We're at a crucial moment." There was no way I was going to disobey her; I would actually slip into a coma if I had to sit here for another hour.

"So you know your lines for today?" Art asked me.

"Yes," I said, without nodding. "There aren't that many, are there?" Art laughed.

"It's not about how many there are – it's about how you deliver them, how you feel the lines and the scene. In this scene, in the ledge scene, you have to think about all the things that are going on in Polly's head. First of all, she's very scared. She's on a tiny ledge with a drop beneath so big that she can't see the bottom." I swallowed.

"Will there be a mattress or something if I fall off?" I asked him hopefully. "Or a stunt girl?"

"A stunt girl?" Art asked me absently as he concentrated on his notes. "No, Ruby, you only get one of those for the *really* dangerous scenes, explosions and stuff or – if like Imogene – it would cost too much money to replace you."

"OK," I said, trying to hide the anxiety in my voice. I wasn't going to have to act scared. Hanging off a high ledge, even a movie-set ledge, wouldn't require me to act at all.

"Also," Art continued, "Polly still hasn't really understood what's happening to her. This morning she was a prim little English schoolgirl with a clever daddy who loved her and who she loved very much. This afternoon not only has she found out that he's a deranged murderer, but that he never loved her, she is not his daughter and that she is at the very top of the list of people he wants to knock off. She's in shock, she's hurt and confused. She still loves him, even though she's frightened of him. And as for Flame and Gareth trying to persuade her to jump off the ledge and out into nothing so that they can try and catch her hand before she falls? Well, she's only just met them, and ever since they came into her life things have gone terribly wrong. She doesn't trust them and she almost hates Flame. She hates her for telling her the truth. Do you get that?"

"I get it," I said. And I thought I did. I thought about the night Mum and Dad told me they were splitting up and the shock and hurt I felt, not to mention the anger. I was angry because I hadn't wanted to know the truth. I think that was how Polly would be feeling. Almost that she would rather have been led unknowingly to her death on the altar of the evil sorcerer Mordred than find out her daddy didn't love her.

"So," Art said, "when you make that decision to jump, are you doing it because you suddenly realise that Flame is your sister and you trust her?" I shook my head, and Natasha narrowed her eyes at me.

"No," I said. "I'm doing it because the alternative is death. The mummified zombie-witch Morgaine is creeping down towards the ledge and when she gets there she'll take me to be killed anyway. Jumping is the only chance I have. And I'm a survivor. I'm only just beginning to realise how tough I really am after all those years of being brought up as an English rose."

Art nodded.

"Good," he said, patting me heavily on the shoulder. "Good girl."

"Art?" I asked him. "Will there be wires when I jump off the ledge? Like safety wires?"

"Wires?" Art looked at me, puzzled. "You won't need wires, Ruby."

"'kay," I said. And my mouth suddenly went dry.

"Ruby?" Art peered at my face and saw underneath all the make-up and dirt and spray-on sweat that I had gone white as a sheet. "Ruby?" Art asked me. "You do realise, don't you, that the ledge will only be about ten centimetres off the floor?"

"Um, yes?" I said, making it obvious that I didn't.

"Ruby!" Art said gently. "I'm sorry. I forgot this is your first time on any kind of film set, let alone an action film. I'm so sorry. Everything else in this scene is green screen. You know about green screen, right?" he asked me.

I decided that bluffing would only make me look even more stupid than I already did.

"Not really," I said.

The sound stage was nothing like I had imagined. There were all the lights hanging high above me, glistening and sparkling like giant Christmas-tree decorations, and all the camera and sound equipment that I was half-familiar with. That much I had got right. But I had pictured the set for the Caverns of Mordred as being built to scale right here, just as they had built an entire square and mews for *Kensington Heights*. I thought it would be like that but even grander – one huge big set that I could walk on to and act just as if I was in a real secret underground cavern.

Nothing could have been further from the truth. There were only two pieces of set. My ledge, which was, as Art said, about ten centimetres high with a bit of rocky cliff face sheering up behind it. And then about ten metres away and a little higher up there was the other ledge – the ledge Imogene and Harry would be on. The "ravine" in between the cavern's walls and all around weren't there. In those spaces all there was were sheets of bright green material.

"Green screen," Art told me as he led me on to the set a few minutes early. "What I need for you to do, Ruby, is to *imagine* the drop beneath you. *Imagine* the zombie witch crawling towards you and *see* her. It's just the same as imagining how Polly is feeling inside. But you've also got to imagine what she sees around her and how she is reacting to it. And after the film is shot, the computer-generated effects – like the witch, the fire in the depths and all that – will be layered over the top, and then that together with the live action will in turn be dropped against a background painting of the caverns."

"Pete?" Art looked up and called a man with blond hair over. "This is Pete. He's brought you the storyboard for today's scene so you can visualise it."

I looked at the drawings, which were almost like a comic strip. Each part or frame of the scene had been drawn out and planned, including the parts I had to imagine – the ravine, the witch and the fire.

"This helps us position you right for when the effects are added," Art told me. "It's a very precise process. So you know when Polly jumps and Flame doesn't manage to catch her and she falls?" I nodded. "Well, we'll cut as you jump and then morph you into a computer-generated version of you. That will be the you that falls into the pit of fire, thought lost for ever. Are you comfortable with all this, Ruby?"

I looked around me at the huge studio and the blazing lights and the crew all there for me – me, two film stars and a tiny, tiny set.

"I think I can do it," I told Art.

"I *know* you can," Art said.

"Ms Grant and Mr McLean on set!" somebody shouted from behind the cameras.

"All right then," Art said, looking me in the eyes. "This is where the fun begins."

THE LOST TREASURE OF KING ARTHUR©

A WIDE OPEN UNIVERSE PRODUCTION

DIRECTED BY *ART DUBROVNIK*

WRITTEN BY *ART DUBROVNIK* AND *ADRIENNE SCOTT*

STARRING: *IMOGENE GRANT*, *HARRY MCLEAN* AND *SEAN RIVERS*

INT. TIME OF DAY – INDISCERNIBLE, THE SECRET CAVERNS OF MORDRED

POLLY is perched on the edge of a ledge that hangs over a narrow but deep ravine. The bottom is lost in darkness. On the other side of the ravine FLAME and GARETH are waiting for her. POLLY is very distressed and confused.

POLLY

Who are you? Why are you doing this to me? It was just a normal day until you came and told all these lies and now… (POLLY LOOKS OVER HER SHOULDER INTO THE DARKNESS WHERE SHE CAN HEAR STRANGE NOISES GETTING CLOSER.) I hate you! I hate you!

FLAME edges along the ledge and tries to reach across to POLLY who cowers away from her. The gap is just too great and FLAME slips and almost falls; she is caught just in time by

GARETH. Rubble falls and long moments pass before we hear it hit the ground.

FLAME

Please, please believe me.
All I want to do is to
help, to save you. Ember –
you have to trust me!

POLLY

My name is not Ember! I'm
Polly Harris. I have been
all my life, and I… (POLLY
becomes very upset.) I don't
understand any of this. Why
is this happening to me?
I'm just a normal girl.

Suddenly the hissing growl that they have been hearing in the background is very loud. Out of the shadows creeps THE ZOMBIE WITCH MORGAINE. She inches closer to POLLY.

                    MORGAINE
        (Her voice is dry and crypt-like.)
             Come, come my lady Guinivere.
             Let me take you to meet
             your master at last. Ha,
             ha, ha!

POLLY cowers back from MORGAINE as
she approaches her. She is frozen
with fear.

                    FLAME
             Ember! Polly, I mean! Just
             jump, stretch out your arms
             and jump. I swear I'll
             catch you. It's your only
             chance!

POLLY looks from MORGAINE to FLAME.
She jumps.

"Action!"

Chapter Ten

'...And it was just *amazing*," I told Danny, Nydia and Anne-Marie as we sat in the café. It was my first Saturday off, the first time we had all been together since I had started on the film a week earlier.

"We know," Anne-Marie said, rolling her eyes. I looked at her quizzically.

"How could you know?" I asked her.

"Because according to you," Danny said, leaning towards me and smiling his heart-flipping smile, "every single thing you do there is 'amazing'. You've said 'amazing' about two hundred times so far this morning, don't you reckon, Nydia?"

Nydia glanced up from her cup of tea which she had been stirring for at least a minute and smiled a half-smile.

"At least," she said, before going back to stirring her tea. I looked at her. She was quiet, not like Nydia at all. Not like Nydia used to be. Since the auditions for *The*

Lost Treasure of King Arthur she seemed to have made herself smaller. I missed her loud laughs and her endless questions and mad ideas. She was here but not here all at once.

"Not like you to have tea, Nydia," I said, licking the whipped cream that topped my hot chocolate off the teaspoon. "Sure you don't want a choccy marshmallow special? I'll buy you one." Nydia shook her head.

"I want tea," she said firmly. I glanced questioningly at Anne-Marie who pulled down the corners of her mouth and gave a little shrug. I thought of the talk Nydia and I had had in the corridor just before I left to start on the film. About how unhappy she felt. She had told me that everything was fine just before I went, but I knew that it wasn't. It wasn't, and for some reason she didn't want to admit it or talk to me about it. I took a sip of my hot chocolate and felt the warm sweetness on the back of my tongue. Hot chocolates in the café were a tradition for me and Nydia, long before we made friends with Anne-Marie and I somehow got Danny as my boyfriend – back when it sometimes seemed that it was me and Nydia against the world. About a million years before I got the part of Polly Harris, a part Nydia wanted and probably deserved much more than I did because she didn't mess up her first audition. She was brilliant in her first audition.

But it looked as if our hot-chocolate tradition was over, and I worried that those years and years of friendship were changing for ever too. I didn't want that to happen. I had to stop it and find some way of getting Nydia back again. After all, not so long ago we had been so close we had practically been twins.

I listened as Anne-Marie chatted on about some scandal at school with Menakshi Shah and Michael Henderson ("As if *he'd* ever go out with *her* when he's still in love with *me*...") and glanced out the window where two girls of around ten had been hovering for the last five minutes or so, as if wondering whether or not to come in. I smiled to myself; they reminded me of Nydia and I a few years ago, wanting to come into the café by ourselves and be grown up, but looking carefully at the menu to see what we could afford. These two were doing exactly the same thing, only they were taking a lot longer about it and giggling like crazy every few minutes.

"What about school work?" Anne-Marie asked me, sipping the cappuccino which she didn't really like but had ordered to be cool. "What's it like working with a tutor? Nightmare of the total variety, right?" I thought for a moment.

"Well," I said, "it's all right. My tutor is called Fran Francisco and I have to call her Fran, and it's her full-time job to keep kids on film sets up with their school work, no matter where they're from or what they study. So she sort of knows a bit about everything. And when Sean Rivers comes she'll be doing the same for him, only American high-school stuff, I suppose. I don't know if it's very different but..." Anne-Marie pretended to faint, and half-slid down the back of her chair.

"Do you mean that you are going to be in the same class as Sean Rivers?" she asked, clutching her hand over her heart. "Oh my gosh, imagine that, sitting next to Sean Rivers! You both reach for a biro at the same time... your hands accidentally touch... a thrill of electricity runs between you... you look up at each other... your eyes lock and..."

I looked at Danny whose sweet smile was rapidly disappearing under a stormy cloud.

"Probably won't be," I said. "Shouldn't think I'll see him at all when I'm not on set."

"But you see 'Imogene' and 'Jeremy' all the time off set," Anne Marie said, doing an annoyingly good impression of me as she mentioned the actors' names. "You haven't stopped banging on about them since you got back."

It was true that I had spent a lot more time with the stars that I had ever imagined. Imogene was the biggest surprise; she was so friendly and always ready to talk if we had waiting time between takes or scenes. At first I had been in awe of her, and then as we talked about how she had started out or worked through scenes together, I would sort of forget who she was until I'd look up suddenly, or catch her reflection in a mirror, and she would be Imogene Grant, international movie star again. Then my mouth would go dry and I had to pinch myself hard to make myself realise how amazing it was to be acting with her. Amazing – I *had* started to use that word a lot.

But it *was* amazing because Imogene always had time for me. She invited me to her Winnebago for tea, let me look at her photos and told me stories about all the people she'd worked with. Or sometimes we just talked about films we liked or books we had read. We both loved *Anne of Green Gables* – we talked about that for hours.

Until I met Imogene I had sort of thought that all incredibly famous people would be divas – a bit like Brett Summers used to be before she was fired from *Kensington Heights* for throwing tantrums and acting like the centre of the universe – but a hundred times worse. Always going everywhere with hundreds of helpers, bossing people around and demanding a dressing room full of white flowers and French bottled water served at precisely one degree below room temperature, and instantly firing anyone who got it wrong.

I had thought Imogene might be like that, but the only help she had was her PA Clarice, who she treated like a best friend, and her dog Muttley, a black Labrador cross who went everywhere with her. Sometimes her mobile phone would ring when I was with her and she'd look at the number and say, "Ruby, do you mind if I take this?" And of course I'd go away so she could talk to whoever it was in private. And once I glanced back and saw her talking and laughing and twiddling her hair and fluttering her lashes and I thought that whoever was calling her must be someone she was in love with.

I didn't ask her who because she is famous for keeping her private life private and would never sell photos of her wedding to magazines for millions of pounds like *some* people I could mention, which, let's face it, is just not classy.

And I *did* see a lot of Jeremy – because we had a lot of scenes together and he was a perfectionist. So we rehearsed and rehearsed them between takes. And even when Art thought we had a scene in the can, Jeremy would sometimes ask to do it again because he thought he could do it even better. And I didn't mind working like that. I didn't mind because just by watching and listening to Jeremy I felt I was learning from him. Acting with him was like nothing else I had ever done. All the other actors I had worked with were either kids from school, who were all great but still beginners like me, or soap actors. And sometimes soap actors are amazing and sometimes they are on a sort of autopilot and just going through the motions in front of a camera.

But Jeremy was always switched on, always in the moment. And I believe in him so much that when we shot the scene where Professor Darkly is stalking towards me about to cut out my heart with the Sacred Knife of Avalon, my heart really was pounding in terror, my mouth really was dry, and when I looked around me all I could see was a dark chamber with no way out, and not the green screens at all. When Art shouted cut there were tears streaming down my face and I hadn't even known I was crying. We didn't need to do any more takes for that scene. Afterwards, Jeremy, back to himself again in an instant, came up to me and gave me a fatherly hug.

"Oh, Ruby," he said. "You're going to be brilliant one day."

If anyone else had said that to me I might have been offended by it, but when he said it I felt – well – *amazing*.

And the other nice thing about Jeremy was that he put up with my mum hanging around without showing that he minded at all. In fact, when I had a scene and he didn't, he even let Mum go for lunch with him, twice. Mum couldn't stop talking about him and about what a gentleman he was and how funny and polite, and she got quite silly and her voice went high, and I know that she really wants to get back with Dad and hasn't got time to waste on a silly crush at her age, so I told her about Jeremy's supermodel girlfriend Carenza Slavchenkov who is much younger (and thinner) than her, and she calmed down a lot after that. She might have even been a bit sad, but if anyone knows about having crushes on people who will never like them back it's me. Before Danny, I was a world expert. I used to have a terrible one on Justin de Souza, and I don't want Mum to get hurt again, not so soon after Dad going. It's my job to look after her now, and telling her about Carenza Slavchenkov was me doing that.

Of course, when I meet Sean Rivers I might have a little wobble myself, but if I do I shall think about Mum and Danny and treat him with professional courtesy only.

I glanced over Danny's shoulder where there were now four girls outside the window dithering about whether or not to come in and finding the whole thing hilarious. Danny on the other hand looked like someone had just told him the worst joke in the world.

"Well, I have spent quite a lot of time with Imogene and Jeremy," I said slowly, "but that's because I have a lot of scenes with them. I have hardly any with Sean," I said, wondering if that was exactly true as I had about one hundred and eight – not that I had counted them or anything. "I mean, for most of time I'm in the film," I went on, "he's getting crushed to death in the Ancient Stone Chamber of Doom, where the walls close in on the prisoner – triggered whenever someone tries to take the Holy Grail from its secret resting place. And anyway," I said, tapping the palms of my hands down on the table top, "even *I'm* bored of me now. Lets talk about you lot. What have you been up to?

"Oh, I know, Nydia – what about your audition for *Holby*? Did you get it?" Nydia looked at each of us.

"I did," she said.

"Hooray!" I yelled, leaping out of my chair and flinging my arms around her. I suppose I was so keen to be happy for her that I maybe overreacted a bit, especially considering that Nydia didn't seem as excited as I did.

"Nydia!" Anne-Marie said. "I didn't even know you'd been for an audition. I can't believe you didn't tell me... Brilliant!"

"It's a proper speaking part and everything," I said.

"Oh, great." Anne-Marie pretended to be miserable. "That's it, I am now officially the only one of us without a part in anything!"

"That's great, Nydia," Danny said. "What's your disease – is it going to make us cry or feel sick?" Nydia shrugged her shoulders a little and I released her from my hug.

"Early onset diabetes caused by morbid obesity," she said. "There's a complication and I die."

"Oh," Anne-Marie said, and then, "wow..."

"You're going to be great, Nyds," Danny said, ignoring the atmosphere that seemed to form around the table. "The actors on that show are really great and so will you be." I sat back down in my chair feeling quite foolish.

"I bet your mum's pleased," I said. Nydia nodded.

"Actually," she said slowly, "she's having a sort of party for me next Friday. She said to invite all of you. You will come, won't you? Because otherwise it will just be aunties and uncles and cousins and... I didn't even want a party, but you know Mum. She makes a big deal out of everything."

"Well, it is a big deal," I said.

"Oh, yes!" Anne-Marie said excitedly. "We'll be there, won't we, Danny? And I can get Menakshi, Jade and that lot to come and if they come then so will the boys and... Hey!" Anne-Marie clicked her fingers. "Ruby can bring Sean Rivers!" she said, bouncing in her seat. "If word gets round that Sean Rivers is going to be at your party, Nydia, then everyone will come." Anne-Marie giggled. "I'll spread the word."

"No!" Nydia looked upset. "No, I don't want a big party! I just want you three there. *You* will be there, won't you, Ruby? That's all I want. I don't want loads of people from school knowing about the part. I'll just get so much aggro for it and it won't air for weeks so I might as well put it off until then. Please, just promise me that you will be there."

"I'll be there," Danny and Anne-Marie said all at once. I bit my lip and looked out of the window where the group of girls had increased to ten or eleven; they must be some kind of Brownie group or something, about to go on a trip out. I looked at Nydia. Strictly speaking I didn't know if I would be working next Friday or not but I also knew I couldn't let her down. Whatever my hours were next week I had to make her party and show that she was still important to me.

"Of course I'll be there," I said.

"Really?" she asked me. I was worried by how surprised she sounded.

"Of course," I said. "It's my best friend's party – I'm not going to miss that for the world." Nydia smiled at me and it was the first real expression I had seen on her face all morning.

"Good," she said, lowering her voice just for me, "because I really need—"

"Oh my word." Anne-Marie cut across Nydia and the expression on her face made both Nydia and I turn to where she was looking, over Danny's shoulder and out of the café window.

"Danny…" I said in slow disbelief. "You'd better turn round very, very slowly."

Outside the window where the group of girls had been gradually growing there now stood about twelve. They stood in a long line, each one of them holding part of a banner that looked like it had been hastily made by taping several bits of A4 together. Scrawled on this banner in a variety of coloured felt tips were the words:

WE ♡ U DANNY HARVEY!

As Danny turned round and the girls caught a glimpse of his face they started to jump up and down and scream.

"Blimey," Danny said, his face turning white.

"It's a mob!" Anne-Marie laughed. "Danny, you're being mobbed by little girls."

Danny turned to me and as he reached for my hand twelve girls booed enthusiastically.

"What am I going to do?" he asked, leaning close to me, which got the girls booing again. I thought for a moment.

"Well," I said, "even when I was on *Kensington Heights* I never had anything like this, but Justin did. And he would just go out and be polite and sign autographs and chat and everyone would be happy. I think the best thing to do would be for us to go out and for you to... greet your public." I couldn't resist a tiny smile.

"Ruby!" Danny said, a bloom of embarrassment colouring his cheeks again. "This isn't funny – I mean Justin loves all this sort of thing. It's not really my scene..."

"We could creep out of the back door," Anne-Marie suggested, looking at the group of girls who were now chanting "We love Danny!" with some distaste. Mr Hollinghurst, the café owner, came over to our table and leaned over Danny's shoulder.

"I'm terribly sorry, 'sir'," he said, clearly having

trouble calling a thirteen-year-old boy sir. "But your –
ah – 'fans' are blocking the entrance and putting off
customers. I'm going to have to ask you to leave."
Danny looked back at the girls, who screamed
whenever he moved. Mr Hollinghurst looked with a
sort of muted astonishment at the mini-mob. "You are
most welcome to use the back door, sir, if you wish."

"Um... right," Danny said, looking at me. "Right,
well... No, no, Ruby's right, I should be nice to them.
I'll just go and sign some autographs and then we can
go home. It will be fine, won't it, Ruby?" he asked,
looking nervously at me.

"Completely fine," I said firmly. "I mean they're
just little girls. How much mobbing can twelve girls
do?"

It's *amazing* how much mobbing twelve girls can do.

I think it would have been fine if they hadn't all
rushed at Danny the moment he stepped out of the
café. And maybe he would have had a chance to sign
autographs if they hadn't pulled his jacket off him
while elbowing me out of the way and trampling on
Anne-Marie and Nydia's feet.

"Why you little…" Anne-Marie yowled. "Right, I've had enough of this!" And I saw her march off as the crowd jostled me.

Some of them grabbed Danny's hair and tried to pull it out. Two began a tug of war on his T-shirt, which ripped after a few moments.

"Look!" I heard Anne-Marie's voice from a few metres away. "It's Sean Rivers!" Not all of the girls looked in Anne-Marie's direction but a few did, and it was just enough for Danny to be able to shake himself loose and break out of the group.

"Run, Danny!" I shouted, but Danny was already running and I followed him as closely as I could, feeling my chest about to explode and hearing my heart thundering in my ears as I pounded after him, finally thankful that my mum made me wear sensible shoes.

We didn't really notice where we were going, Danny and I. We just turned down house-lined street after street until finally the sound of insane girls shouting his name had died away completely.

"That was like some terrible zombie film," Danny said, sitting on a garden wall and leaning over as he caught his breath. "I never knew girls could be so… *hard*."

"They *were* a bit wild," I said, flopping next to him on the wall. "I mean, they went *crazy* – over *you*!"

"Yeah, well," Danny said, giving me a sideways look. "Is it really that surprising?"

"*Yes!*" One look at his face made me correct myself hastily. "I mean *no*, of course not. It's just that I had no idea you had got *that* popular so quickly. That's pop star popular, Danny! If you released a single today it would be number one by the weekend!" I laughed, but Danny looked embarrassed.

"They did actually ask me to record a single," he mumbled, the flush in his cheeks no longer from running so hard in the cold air.

"*Did they?*" I asked, astounded, and then added, "I mean, of course they did. Who's they?" Danny winced and wrinkled his nose.

"The production company," he told me. "They wanted me to sing a version of the *Kensington Heights* theme tune with words. They gave me the lyrics to look at. They are totally slushy, and I said no, but... well, they did ask. They thought it would be a 'smash'. They said I'd had 'instantaneous' appeal or something like that. Liz said older women wanted to mother me and younger girls wanted to go out with me. She's still going on about it, actually – but I can't even sing,

Ruby! And anyway, I want to be a real actor – like Jeremy Fort – not some one-hit wonder or someone only known for his sex appeal."

I was about to laugh but then I realised that Danny wasn't joking.

I stared at my lovely, normal boyfriend and realised that in fact he was not normal at all any more. He had turned into the sort of boy that made girls stupid and giggly, unable to speak properly and prone to forming violent mobs. They felt about him the way I used to feel about Justin de Souza, the way I sort of might feel about Sean Rivers but probably wouldn't, not once I've met him and find out that he's not that nice in real life (hopefully). Which did rather beg the question, what was a genuine heart-throb pin-up of the masses doing going out with me, and how long would it be before he realised he'd made a terrible mistake?

"Well," I said. I knew it was wrong, but I felt a sudden pang of jealousy that surprised me, because it wasn't over all of those girls out there who might be dreaming about Danny and preparing to mob him at that very moment; that made me feel uneasy, but it wasn't that that made me envy him.

I was jealous of Danny and his fame.

When I had been Angel in *Kensington Heights* I had

hated the attention I got – feeling as if my life was under the spotlight all of the time. I had hated it even though the kind of attention I got was nothing like Justin and now Danny get. People didn't write love letters to me, they wrote problem letters. Boys didn't chase me down the street yelling, unless it was with a spider or a frog. Boys never noticed me at all, except to make fun of me – until Danny that is. I hated feeling that I was growing up with everyone looking at me and seeing what a bad job of it I was doing; getting all lumpy and spotty and awkward in front of the whole world. Part of the reason I left the show was to get away from that – to let myself be free to be just me again.

But I hadn't quite realised that the same girls who had used to write to me in their droves would forget me so soon. I hadn't realised that only a couple of months later they'd be trampling over me in their masses to get to my boyfriend without so much as a "Oooh, didn't you used to be Angel MacFarley?"

I never thought that the fame part of being an actor mattered to me. I always thought that as long as I could act I'd be happy wherever it was. But as I realised exactly how famous Danny had become – potential number-one-single-releasing famous – I knew that I missed it. I *missed* fame, and getting my name mentioned every now and then in a magazine didn't really count.

I suddenly saw that when you are not in people's living rooms on their TV every day of the week, or on at the local multiplex, they don't think about you at all. I wanted people to think about me. I wanted to be famous. I wanted it so much just at that moment that it felt like a punch in the stomach. A punch that winded me because I was surprised about how strongly I felt it.

"I can't see you on *Top of the Pops* somehow," I said, forcing the jealousy I was feeling back towards the pit of my tummy.

"If I could sing and play an instrument maybe..." Danny said, sighing heavily. "And then only if I could write my own stuff, and I can't." He hung his head and stared at the cracks in the pavement. "But all this? Girls chasing me and stuff? I don't want this, Rube. I'm not into fame. I just want to act. That's all I want to do. Maybe I should leave *Kensington Heights*."

I picked up his hand and held it. For one sharp moment I wanted him to leave *Kensington Heights* too, but not for his sake – for mine. I wanted *my* Danny back again, all to myself. The first ever boy to think that I was worth noticing. But it was only one moment before I realised that I wanted Danny to have the best chance at a career he could, and I knew that *Kensington Heights* would give him a brilliant chance. After all, if it hadn't been for the show there was no way Art Dubrovnik would have called me back for a second audition. Whether or not that was right or wrong, it was true.

"No," I said. "Don't do that. You've got to stay for at least one season. Look at what working on the show's done for me." Danny nodded.

"That's right," he said, smiling at me. "Here I am feeling all sorry for myself and you've got all this to come and worse. Once you're a movie star the whole world will be in love with you – not just me."

I froze, looking at Danny, with my mouth open. No one had ever said anything that sweet to me ever in my entire life, not even in a script.

Danny and I had spent a lot of time with each other since we started going out in the summer, almost every day. He was a regular part of my group now. We had so much fun together; just having Danny sitting next to me during the most boring maths lesson made it a thousand times less boring. It was obvious to everyone how well we got on. But not once, not even that time I went camping with Danny, his dad and little brother and Danny took me for a walk under the stars and it was so romantic, had either of us used the word "love". Not even indirectly the way that Danny just had.

Somehow I knew it was more than just a casual comment; I knew that Danny really meant to say it, and that made me feel wonderful. The trouble was that I had no idea how to respond.

I tried to think of something to say, to show Danny that I felt the same, but I couldn't. I just gaped, unable to speak. As Danny watched me his sweet, shy smile faded, and he looked down and sort of shrugged as if he could shake what he had said away. He had just said the sweetest, most romantic thing ever to me and all I had done was gawp at him.

"And anyway," he said, keen to kick-start a conversation between us again, "Liz will get some new teenagers in soon enough and no one will notice me any more." He smiled at me as he pushed himself off the garden wall and gestured for me to follow him. All as if I hadn't just blown the most romantic moment of my short life sky high.

"Exactly!" I said, stupidly trying so hard to be bright and breezy.

"Well, come on then, Ruby Parker, film star," Danny said as I fell into step beside him. "I'll walk you home."

And he did. But he didn't hold my hand once the whole way there.

Kensington Heights
(You take me to...)

Words and Music by *Simon Yates*

Before I met you, I was
on a dark and dusty shelf.
Oh and I hated myself
cos I was all alone.

And then you came along
and gave me back my shine
when you told me you'd be
mine
on the telephone.

*And now, your love lifts
me,
so high and so easily,
and I know I'll love you
with all of my might,
because you
take me to –
Kensington Heights.*

And when I'm with you I
know everything's all
right.
The sun will still be
bright
as long as you're here.

And when I'm in your arms
I feel so safe.
Just looking at your face
brings heaven so near.

*And now, your love lifts
me,*
so high and so easily,
and I know I'll love you
with all of my might,
because you
take me to –
Kensington Heights.

Kensington Heights…
Kensington Heights!
(repeat to fade)

"Action!"

Chapter Eleven

"Wow!" I said as Nydia finished singing the words to the *Kensington Heights* theme tune. "Your voice is amazing. You make even those words sound great!"

I had phoned Nydia as soon as I got in from saying goodbye to Danny because I wanted to tell her what had happened: what he had said to me and what I hadn't said to him. I half expected her to say she didn't want to come over so I was glad when she said she would come round straight away.

She shrugged and handed me the lyric sheet.

"Danny brought them into school last week to see what we thought." I looked at the song lyrics. When Nydia had sung them, with her powerful melodious voice, they sounded fantastic. Nydia could make anything sound incredible – she had a brilliant voice. But I couldn't imagine Danny singing them, because as lovely as he was he was right – he couldn't sing.

"He didn't tell me anything about being asked to make

a single when we spoke on the phone last week," I said, laying the lyrics down on my bed.

"Perhaps he couldn't get a word in," Nydia said. She was smiling but I got the feeling she wasn't entirely joking. And it was true – whenever I had spoken to Danny during the week I hadn't really stopped talking about what was happening to me, me, me. I thought about our awkward and near-silent walk home. I still couldn't believe that he had said something so lovely to me and all I had managed to do was make him feel awkward and embarrassed. I didn't want him to think I didn't feel the same, because I did. But I didn't know how to say it. I hadn't exactly had any practice. And now it looked like I wouldn't get to see him and make things OK again until my next days off. He had seemed fine when we'd said goodbye, just like old Danny again. But I couldn't help feeling that things weren't completely right between us; I was sure that I had somehow hurt him.

"Anyway," Nydia continued. "We all agreed they weren't really Danny."

"You should do it," I said. "Seriously, Nydia. You made that sound brilliant."

"Yes," Nydia said sharply, flopping down on my bed next to me. "But I don't think I've got the right looks, do you?"

I put the song sheet down.

"You're still feeling bad, aren't you?" I asked her. "About your weight and everything?" Nydia shrugged. "Is that why you don't want a big party even though you've got three episodes of *Holby City*, which most of the kids at school would kill for?"

"They'd kill to play Polly Harris in *The Lost Treasure of King Arthur*. No one would kill to play a morbidly obese diabetic with a heart problem," Nydia said glumly. "Everyone calls me names at school already. I don't want to give them something else to laugh at," she said miserably. "It'll be bad enough when it goes on air. That's why I've got to lose weight before then. If I'm still fat in six weeks then my life might as well be over..."

"Nydia," I said, "you're not fat – you know you're really beautiful and—"

"Oh, shut up, Ruby," Nydia snapped at me. "I'm not beautiful. You know that I'm not, so don't even try and lie! I am fat and bulbous and ugly and that's that."

"You are not ugly!" I protested, and I wasn't lying. I really did think that Nydia was beautiful.

"Anyway, it doesn't matter," Nydia said, "because I'm just going to lose weight and it won't be an issue any more." I nodded. I wasn't an expert, but Nydia made it sound much easier than I thought it was.

"Did you talk to the nurse then?" I asked her. "About a healthy-eating plan?" Nydia shook her head.

"No," she said. "If I ask the nurse then Mum will know and I don't want her interfering. She'll make a huge big fuss out of it – the whole family will know, all my cousins and my grannies too. And my brother will tease and tease me... so, no." As Nydia had been talking her voice had been steadily growing louder and now she stopped and took a breath. "I found this website about nutrition and exercise and stuff called 'getskinnyquick.com' on the net. It's really good and tells you exactly what to do to lose weight quickly." I smiled tentatively at her; it was sort of hard to know how Nydia was going to react these days.

"Are you sure you don't want to tell your mum?" I suggested. "Tell her it's a girl thing. Ask her to keep it from everyone else. I bet she'd really like to help, if you let her."

Nydia shrugged. "She'd just take over," she said, shrugging as if it wasn't important. "I want to do it by myself."

"Why?" I asked her uneasily.

"Because Mum loves cooking," Nydia said, picking up a cushion and pummelling it as she spoke. "She loves food. She always makes us stay at the table until we clear our plate. She's always giving me snacks – when I get in from school or before I go to bed. If I ask her to help me she'll think I'm blaming her for being the way I am."

I thought for a moment. "Well..." I said carefully, "maybe she is a bit to blame..."

"No! She is not!" Nydia said. "No one else in my family is like this, are they? I'm the only fat one! So it can't be Mum's food, can it? It must just be me being too greedy. I'm disgusting – always stuffing my face. Well not any more. I'm going to do what this website says and I'll just throw away the snacks and stuff Mum gives me without her knowing. And when I lose weight, Mum will think it's just me losing my puppy fat, which she's always saying I'm going to do, and she won't be upset."

Nydia took a breath and I could see from the set of her face that she was really determined. "I just want to do it on my own, Ruby – OK? I haven't told anyone, not even Anne-Marie. I've told you because you're supposed to be my best friend. So promise you won't tell, OK?" I nodded, but Nydia's secrecy made me feel uneasy. It was just the sort of thing I used to tell girls who wrote to me, to go straight to an adult and tell them about it. But I didn't think that disagreeing with Nydia right then would help, so I decided I'd just wait and see what happened, for now.

"OK," I said, conjuring up a reassuring smile. "I promise I won't tell anyone."

Just at that moment Mum knocked on my bedroom door and came in with some juice and a plate of biscuits.

"Here you go, girls," she said, setting the tray down on my dressing table.

"Thanks, Mum," I said, looking longingly at the biscuits.

"Did I hear you singing, Nydia?" Mum said, beaming at us. "You have such a lovely voice. Really wonderful. Maybe you'll be a pop star one day. Like the Jo-lay!"

"J Lo, Mum," I sighed, rolling my eyes at Nydia. "And she's a person not a band."

"Thanks, Mrs Parker," Nydia said, her usual bright self again. "Maybe I will!"

When Mum had shut the door Nydia's smile vanished in an instant. I lifted the juice off the tray and took the plate of biscuits over to my wastepaper bin. Taking one last look at the chocolate digestives I tipped them all in and then stuffed some old magazine on top of them.

"Thank you," Nydia said.

"That's all right," I said, sitting next to her on the bed. I handed her a glass of juice and she took a small sip.

"And you will come to my party next Friday, won't

you, Ruby? Mum will have all these cakes and crisps and stuff, and I know that if you're there I'll be good."

I put my arm around her. "I promise you I'll be there," I said, giving her a little dig in the ribs, "to eat all the cakes and crisps."

"It's not funny," Nydia said, without cracking a smile. "I need you."

Chapter Twelve

"Action!"

It's funny how the most important moments of your life – or at least the moments you always *imagine* will be the most important moments of your life – never turn out like you think they should.

For example, I had rehearsed and rehearsed the moment I was going to meet Sean Rivers both in my head and out loud when nobody was looking, so that if I did accidentally fancy him – and let's face it the probability was high – I could come across as being cool and disinterested, polite but not impressed. I had practised my handshake, a neat incline of my head, and had said over and over again in a calm and sophisticated voice, "I'm Ruby Parker, terribly pleased to meet you."

I knew that I would be rehearsing my first scene with him on my first morning back at work in the second week of filming. Our first scene was when his character, Catcher, tells my character, Polly, the truth about her life while in the Egyptian section of the British Museum. For once we had a proper set to work on with loads of props and things, mainly about twenty fake Egyptian mummies in glass cases, which were really cool, especially the ones that the special-effects man Pete had made to look exactly like Art Dubrovnik.

So I had prepared and prepared for the moment that Art would introduce me to America's hottest teen sensation Sean Rivers, the real-life poster boy of a nation of girls' romantic hopes, until I thought I was ready. In fact, I thought I was so ready that if there had been an Oscar category for "Best display of the least amount of excitement when meeting your favourite heart-throb in a supporting role" I would definitely have won it.

It was more important than ever that I didn't go all silly and have a stupid crush on Sean Rivers because, first of all, Art Dubrovnik thought I was going to and that was just embarrassing. And second of all, even though Danny and I spent Sunday together and Mum cooked us lunch and Dad came over in the afternoon and Danny was as sweet and as funny as he ever was, it felt like things were different between us. Our goodbye under the streetlamp wasn't nearly as comfortable and as happy as it usually was, and when I watched him walk off into the evening, this time without turning round once, I had the feeling that I wanted to call him back, that there was something I had to tell him but just couldn't quite find the words to say.

But I didn't.

I just watched him disappear into the shadows feeling as if, with each moment that passed, our lives were changing a little bit more and the spaces between us were getting bigger.

There are plenty of people ready to line up and say that a thirteen-year-old girl's feelings about her boyfriend aren't remotely important, probably not real and will be forgotten within six months. But I disagree. Whatever happens in six months or six years or sixty, whether I'm married to Danny or on my fifth husband like Brett Summers, I'll always remember one thing – the way I felt on that evening as I said goodbye to Danny for another week. The emotions that were churning around inside my thirteen-year-old skin were as real and as important as anything I will ever feel in my life. And I didn't want Danny to stop being my boyfriend just because I couldn't make him understand how much I care about him.

So I had to show him I wasn't in the least bit bothered about Sean Rivers, even if he was the most famous and best-looking fifteen-year-old in the world.

And after a whole night of rehearsing and a long morning of practising not being in the least bit bothered, I thought I was ready at last.

I knew when I was going to meet him; Art had called us for a read-through and rehearsal before we shot the museum scene that afternoon. Normally all that kind of thing would have been done weeks before, but they had cast Polly's part so late that I hadn't got to do any of it.

I had twenty minutes or so before the rehearsal was due to start, so I left Mum and Jeremy talking enthusiastically about some old relic of a movie called *Brief Encounter* and wandered off to find a quiet place to have a final how-to-react-when-meeting-Sean-Rivers rehearsal.

Wardrobe was empty; all of the staff must have gone for a quick coffee in the lull before the storm, when their boss and chief wardrobe mistress Tallulah Banks would be frightening them all into action.

I looked at my costume rack and the thirty-two sets of the same outfit hanging all the way along it, except for the very last scene of the film – a beach party where I got to wear a swimsuit and a sarong. (The thought of which made me feel more afraid than *really* hanging off a ledge hundreds of metres in the sky.)

I walked past Imogene's rack, which was more or less the same as mine: a row of identical cut-off jeans and a row of white T-shirts, each progressive number a little more dirty and ripped up than the last. Except that Imogene had one other costume for a scene she hadn't shot yet, right at the beginning of the film. It's when her character Flame is at a ball held in the Louvre in Paris, and she's wearing this amazing gold Chanel gown and is acting like a really beautiful librarian, when suddenly art terrorists storm the gallery and try to steal the *Mona Lisa*. Flame goes all woman-action-hero and fights them off single-handed in her gold dress. It's a really great scene and a really, *really* great dress.

I ran my hand over the clear cellophane that protected it and wished that I got to wear a dress like that instead of just an increasingly grubby school uniform. I glanced over my shoulder. There was no one around and the corridor was quiet and I still had a few moments left before I was due at rehearsal, so I lifted the hanger off the rail and held the dress up against me. I walked over to the full-length mirror that was screwed to the wall and looked at my reflection. It was hard to get the full effect through the cellophane, but as I never have been very good at breaking rules, I was too scared to take the dress out of its wrapper, let alone actually try it on. As I swished and swirled in front of the mirror the cellophane creaked and crackled.

"I'm Ruby Parker," I said to the mirror in my haughty meeting-Sean-Rivers voice. "Terribly pleased to meet you." I smiled my practice smile and did a little bow, making the plastic rustle like a bag of crisps.

"I beg your pardon?" I asked my reflection in the mirror, imagining I was looking at Sean himself. "What did you say your name was? Sean Rivers? Never heard of you, I'm afraid." I was like a little girl playing dressing-up, twirling around so that the cellophane-covered material swished around my legs, forgetting to listen for the sound of Tallulah's metal-tipped high heels clicking up the corridor, or anyone else approaching.

"Ah yes, Sean Rivers," I told the mirror in my poshest voice as I did a cellophane-covered curtsey. "It is an honour for *you* to meet *me*, Ruby Parker."

"Hey and I believe you," the real Sean Rivers said from behind me. "And by the way – nice twirl."

I sort of yelped in surprise, and as I whirled around the long hem of the dress got caught under the heel of my trainer. Even as it happened, even as I tumbled on to the floor and heard the horrible sound of gold silk ripping and collapsed in a heap at Sean Rivers' feet looking like a total idiot, I was thinking, *Of course this is how you are going to meet Sean Rivers. You are Ruby Parker after all. Things never go the way you think they will.*

He smiled down at me.

"Need a hand?" he asked me, crouching down and cocking his head to one side to look at me as if I were a curious museum exhibit. "Are you OK, Ruby Parker?"

I braced myself for heart failure, but somehow it seemed that Sean Rivers' smile, though extremely nice and very handsome, wasn't as fatal as I had feared. It was more likely the humiliation would kill me, I decided, red in the face and tangled up in a gown worth thousands of pounds, which I had probably ruined.

And then it struck me: it wouldn't be the embarrassment that finished me off – it would be Tallulah Banks who would murder me as soon as she found out what I'd done.

"I think I'm going to get the sack," I told Sean Rivers, marvelling at the fact that my voice came out normal and that I could string a sentence together. It had to be the shock, I decided. As soon as I got back to normal I'd go all silly and flappy over him just as expected.

Sean laughed and took my hand. Anne-Marie would have been interested to know that there was no surge of electricity at his touch. He helped me up on to my knees and between us we carefully eased the gown out from around my legs. In the distance I heard metal-tipped footsteps clacking down the corridor.

"Oh no!" I whispered urgently. "It's Tallulah Banks! She's going to kill me!" Sean grinned and his blue eyes twinkled, but I was sure that the only reason my heart was beating so quickly was the fear of getting caught by Tallulah Banks.

"It'll be cool, Ruby Parker," Sean said. "Trust me."

We stood up and brushed ourselves down. Sean hung the dress back on the rack.

"Just act natural," he whispered. "When she comes we act natural, and no one knows anything about any ripped dress – right? It could be weeks before that costume is used and by then there'll be no evidence to pin it on you."

"You sound like you get into these situations a lot," I said to Sean. He winked at me.

"Let's just say I like to liven up a shoot wherever I can, otherwise I'd go crazy." Sean crossed his eyes as he said the last word, forcing me to clap my hand over my mouth to stifle a laugh as Tallulahs steps got ever closer.

"Compared to the trouble I've seen, Ruby Parker," Sean told me, "you are an amateur. Ready?"

"Ready," I said as Tallulah the wardrobe mistress turned into the room.

"What are you two doing in here?" she asked us smartly, flaring her nostrils so that her nose ring quivered. For a relatively young woman she was exceptionally scary. I thought of Lisa telling me how Tallulah never forgets and never forgives someone messing up her carefully-run wardrobe department, and I think my knees actually knocked.

"Hi! Sean Rivers." Sean reached out to shake Tallulah's limp, cold hand. "Very pleased to meet you, I've been—"

"I know who you are," Tallulah said, withdrawing her hand from his, utterly unimpressed. "What I want to know is what you are doing in here..."

"Oh, nothing really. I'm new on set so Ruby was just showing me—" Sean started.

"I was looking at the gold dress and I ripped it," I blurted out before he could finish. Sean raised an eyebrow but said nothing.

"I can't help it," I told him with a shrug. "I'm really bad at rebelling. Always have been."

Tallulah narrowed her black-lined eyes at me before sweeping up to where the dress hung and dragging the cellophane into a bunch around the hanger. Her appraisal was swift and deadly.

"It's a rip in the hem," she told me, pulling the cellophane down over the gown with a sharp, whip-like crack. "Fortunately for you I can repair it and no one will notice. But I have no choice but to tell Mr Dubrovnik all about this. This dress is worth thousands of pounds. We're supposed to be giving it back! My department is the essential core of this production, not a glorified dress-up box for you little movie brats!" Tallulah spat the words out like an angry cat. "Without me, without my costumes, you have nothing. Do you understand?"

"Yes, Tallulah," I said meekly. Sean was not so meek. He crossed his arms and raised one eyebrow.

"So tell me..." he asked her with casual insolence. "What would you do with your costumes if you didn't have actors to put them on?" Tallulah Banks opened and shut her mouth in indignation.

"Don't you cheek me, young man," she told Sean. "I don't care who you are, I don't care if you're Prime Minister. When you're in my wardrobe department you follow *my* rules, and you don't mess with *me*. And another thing—"

"Boring, boring, boring," Sean interrupted her.

I stared at him and held my breath waiting for Tallulah's tirade to gather speed. But before she could utter a word Sean grabbed my hand.

"Run!" he yelled, yanking me towards the door. "Run for it, Ruby, she's gonna blow!"

So me and Sean Rivers ran, laughing like lunatics, through the corridors towards the rehearsal room as fast as we could until we couldn't hear Tallulah Banks shouting, "Come back here RIGHT NOW!" at us any more. We stopped a few metres from the rehearsal room to catch our breath.

"Ruby Parker," Sean said between breaths. "It really is an honour to meet you. I can tell you are going to be fun to know." I laughed and held out my hand for Sean to shake.

"Terribly pleased to meet you," I said, and we both laughed again.

Art Dubrovnik came around the corner, followed by Lisa and the clipboard which seemed to be a permanent part of her anatomy.

"I see you two have met," he said as he swept past us. "Remember what I said, Ruby? No falling in love."

He and Lisa walked into the room leaving Sean and I standing in the corridor looking at each other.

"He's joking," I told Sean hurriedly. "I'm not going to fall in love with you at all. How ridiculous. It's just his little joke." And as I said it I realised that it was true. As tall and as good-looking and as fun as Sean Rivers definitely was, I hadn't gone all stupid over him just like I, and everybody else in the world apparently, had expected me to.

It was funny, but it never occurred to me that the way I felt about Danny might actually withstand meeting the world's best-looking boy, or that my relationship with Danny was stronger than a silly crush. But now that I realised it was, now I realised I could work with Sean Rivers and like him without it being compulsory to fall in love with him, I felt incredible relief. My life was going to be a lot less complicated than I had predicted – for once.

Sean shrugged.

"Of course you're not in love with me. And you know what?" Sean clapped a hand on my shoulder as we walked into the room behind Art. "I like that about you, Ruby Parker. You have no idea how boring it is to have girls falling in love with you at first sight."

Chapter Thirteen

"Action!"

Sean Rivers was fantastic.

I had the best fun I have had since I started working on the film the moment that he arrived. The other main actors, Imogene and Jeremy and Harry, were all really nice but there are two essential differences between them and Sean Rivers: they are properly old and Sean is fifteen. Which is old enough to be cooler than me, but – in Sean's case anyway – not so old as to be too cool to hang out with thirteen-year-old me. And while Imogene and the other adult actors take acting really, really seriously, Sean just wants to have fun. And somehow, while he's having fun, he acts really, really well. And it's as effortless as a dolphin in water; it's his natural environment. At least that's what I thought at first.

Between takes on our second day of working together when we were hanging about on the edge of the set, Sean told me he never even wanted to act, he actually wanted to be a bus driver, when he was discovered shopping with his mum on Fifth Avenue in

New York at the age of eight. A talent scout for a model agency thought he had the kind of cute and cheeky good looks she needed for a new children's-wear campaign she was casting. The next thing Sean knew he was shooting a commercial. "I didn't know what was happening. The more I messed around in front of a camera, the more they loved me," he told me. "They said I was a natural. A natural fool, my mom said."

Then he got noticed by some Hollywood producers who screen-tested him for his first film co-starring with a Great Dane called Ernest, *Doggy's Day Out*. And the rest is a history that I know quite well, as I have a Sean Rivers scrapbook with lots of magazine clippings about him glued into it – not that I was about to tell him, or in fact anyone, *that* little secret.

"And the thing is, Ruby Parker," he said, gesturing to the set of the British Museum around him, "all of this stuff just happens to me, or at least Dad made it so all this stuff happens to me. I didn't want any of it."

"But you're glad you're doing it, aren't you?" I asked him. He shrugged.

"I guess so," he said uncertainly. His face seemed to cloud over for a moment before his tentative smile broadened into a dazzling grin. "I guess it beats going to school every day."

"Oh, about that," I said. "This afternoon we've got lessons with this tutor called Fran Francisco…"

Sean groaned and flopped face-first on the floor.

"Call a paramedic," he yelled. "I'm dying of boredom!"

I was doubled up with laughter when a long cold shadow fell over both of us.

"What do you think you're doing?" a man's voice said. "Get up at once."

Sean stood up immediately, his smile and easy demeanour utterly gone.

"I'm sorry, sir," he said. I stared at the man who seemed to intimidate Sean so much. I wondered where the Sean who had cheeked a much more frightening Tallulah Banks was hiding. I felt suddenly protective of him.

"Er, excuse me," I said to the man haughtily. I was about to tell him that he had to have a pass to come on set, but Sean stopped me.

"Ruby – this is my father, Patrick Rivers. He's my manager too." Sean smiled weakly at his father. "Dad, this is Ruby Parker."

Patrick Rivers looked at me without smiling.

"I know who you are, and I hope you are not going to distract my son, young lady," he told me. "Sean is here to work. He has got no time for anything else, so don't get any ideas."

"I beg your pardon...?" I was so amazed by his rudeness that I forgot to be intimidated by him. He glowered at me, darkly furious.

"I'm warning you..." he began, his voice almost a growl. I started to feel intimidated, but just at that moment Art appeared from behind part of the scenery and smiled at Mr Rivers.

"Hi, Pat!" He greeted Sean's father as if he were an old friend, but I got the sense that it was a veneer of good will only. "Look, I've got no problem with the kids having fun between takes," he told Sean's dad. "If I did they'd know about it – and besides, your son's giving a hundred per cent on set." Art leaned against a partition wall and smiled easily at Pat Rivers.

"Of course, of course." Patrick Rivers smiled the moment he saw Art, putting his arm around his son, laughing awkwardly. "Just making sure you're getting value for money, Art."

"Well, Pat," Art said, watching Mr Rivers carefully, "you should know – you negotiated his fee!"

Both men gave hearty and entirely fake laughs before Art left to make a few more lighting adjustments. Pat Rivers' arm dropped away from Sean the minute Art was gone.

"I've got calls to make," he told Sean. "Come straight back to the Winnebago when you've finished here. We'll discuss your punishment then."

"Punishment?" I asked Sean in horror after his dad had gone.

Sean shrugged, amazingly his smile was back again as if all that had just happened was a cloud passing over the sun.

"Don't mind him," he told me. "The actual punishment is never usually as bad as you imagine it to be."

"But you didn't do anything wrong!" I said.

"Do you want to tell that to Dad?" Sean asked me, raising both his brows as he said it.

I had to admit that I didn't.

Once the chill of Pat Rivers' on-set visit had thoroughly thawed, the rest of the day flew by. At the end of it Mum, Imogene and Jeremy had gathered to watch us wrap our final scene with Harry.

"Cut!" Art shouted and a ripple of applause went round the studio. Art stood back and looked from me to Sean.

"You two are a good team," he said with approval. "Sparks were really flying there. We took a risk casting Ruby without getting you two together, but it's really working. It really is." Sean and I smiled at each other.

"I'll let PR know," Lisa Wells said, writing a note on her clipboard.

"What can I say?" Sean said, ruffling my hair. "I always wanted a kid sister."

I should have been gutted that the world's most gorgeous teenage boy thought of me as a sister, but I wasn't, I was really happy. Happy that Sean and I liked each other so much that working with him was easy and tension free. And happy that even after meeting him, a boy who I had once daydreamed about marrying, I still wanted Danny to be my boyfriend.

I couldn't wait to tell him and get things back to normal between us again.

"Right," Art said. "Thank you everyone for gathering here for a little meeting. I've got some real work for you to do, I'm afraid."

Everyone groaned except for Imogene and me. She saw the puzzled look on my face and winked at me.

"Imogene's new film, *Lizzie Bennet*, a modern reworking of the classic Jane Austen novel *Pride and Prejudice*, is premiering in the West End on Friday. Of course, Imogene will be there walking the red carpet, and we've decided that all of you should go too, to give her and our film some support."

"To a movie premiere!" I said excitedly. "Brilliant! I can't wait to see it – oh, Imogene, what are you going to wear? Can I help you choose?" Imogene laughed, but before she could answer Art spoke.

"No, you can't," Art said, "because you'll be too busy choosing your own dress, Ruby." He smiled at me. "You can't walk the red carpet in jeans and a T-shirt."

"I... I mean – do you mean me?" I managed to say, looking at Mum, who from the look on her face had already known all about this. "I'm going to walk down the red carpet?"

"I want you all there, the entire lead cast working that carpet, working the press. Let's get a buzz going on the film now, get the media interested in the on-set dynamics. It can never hurt, right, Lisa?"

"Right," Lisa said, busily scribbling away on her pad. "I'll update PR on the news." I was too excited to wonder what news.

"Me walking up a red carpet..." I said in awe. And then I remembered that everyone else in this room (except maybe Lisa, the camera crew and Pete the special-effects man) had done it hundreds of times. "I mean, yeah, of course, I'll be happy to do it," I added, trying to sound normal again. "Whatever."

Sean stifled a laugh beside me and Art gave me quite a hard stare.

"I'm so glad," he said heavily. "Now, it's on Friday, so—"

"Oh, no," I cried. Everyone looked at me.

"What now, Ruby?" Art asked me, a tad impatiently.

"I can't go," I said. Art smiled, but only his mouth moved.

"What do you mean you can't go?" he said.

"It's my friend Nydia's party – do you remember her from the auditions? She was really good – and anyway she got a part in this soap and her mum is doing her a party to celebrate, not a big thing just a few mates, but I promised..." I caught sight of my mum shaking her head at me and making a chopping motion across her mouth, so I stopped talking.

"Ruby," Art said, his voice ever so low, "while you're on my team, my team comes first, do you understand? You're standing on an Art Dubrovnik movie set with some of the world's most talented and powerful actors. I'm sure they've all got better things to do too, but they are all going to the premiere. Do you know why they are going?" Art leaned his face closer to mine as he asked me. "Because they understand that it's their job, and their job comes first. Now you are going to that premiere, Ruby. You're going because you're contracted to fulfil your publicity commitments and you're going because you don't want to let me or your team mates down, do you?" I shook my head slowly.

"No, Art," I said quietly. "Of course I'll go. I'm sorry."

I wondered how I was going to explain to Nydia. At any other time in the past I thought she would have been fine about it, and after all I really wanted to go to the premiere, my first ever one. But at the moment, when she seemed so strange and tense, I was really worried about breaking a promise to her; it seemed so important to her that I was there.

"Don't worry," Sean whispered in my ear. "The premiere will all be over by eight, barring the after-show party. We can go then."

"We?" I whispered back.

"Sure," Sean said. "English kids' party – excellent!"

"Um, the thing is…" I said, wondering if me, Nydia, Anne-Marie, Danny, Nydia's grannies and some snacks really constituted a party worthy of an LA teenager.

"We've got a heavy filming schedule this week," Art continued, "so you'll be getting kitted out tonight. Guys, you'll go with Lisa and Tallulah." All three male cast members groaned. "They're taking you to Paul Smith in Covent Garden." Art turned to my mum and I. "Ruby, Janice – Imogene and Clarice have volunteered to look after you two. Mr Rivers, I'm assuming you can kit yourself out?"

Sean jumped at the mention of his father's name; none of us had realised he had arrived.

"Mum's coming?" I asked, wondering how my coolness factor (which was already in the low ones) would be affected by walking up a red carpet with my mummy.

"Parents are obligatory," Sean told me, faking a yawn. "My dad hates me doing all this stuff, but he knows I have to do it to promote my movies so that I can get more work. Still, if you know what to do, you can usually give parents the slip."

"What about being punished?" I whispered to Sean, feeling genuinely concerned for him. I had never known anybody who was *actually punished* before.

"Ruby, if I didn't break out sometimes," Sean told me, "I'd go crazy. It's worth the risk."

"Ah-hem," Art coughed loudly and narrowed his eyes at us. "You will all be visiting Harrods where you will borrow the dresses of your choice. And then you will go to De Beers in Bond Street where you will choose some jewellery."

"But it's Monday," I said. Art looked blankly at me. "I mean, it's not late-night shopping on a Monday in England." Art was about to say something else when Imogene stepped forward and put her hand on my shoulder.

"Don't worry, Ruby," she said. "Shops have a habit of staying open just for me." I turned my face to look up at her.

"Wow," I said.

"Exactly," she said. "So I'll pick you up in the limo and we'll go shop."

That night a little bit of the glamour and magic that surround Imogene Grant wore off on me and I felt that I really knew what it meant to be a movie star at last, to be the kind of person the whole world stopped for.

When we got to Harrods a smartly-dressed lady was waiting for us by a side entrance. She looked both ways down the street, probably scouting for press, before she opened the limo door and waited for us to climb out.

"Ms Grant," she said. "What a pleasure to have you visit us again."

"Farrah," Imogene said, giving the lady a kiss on her cheek. "Thank you so much for this. This is Ruby Parker and her mother Janice Parker. They'll need gowns too."

"Always happy to oblige," Farrah said. She showed us to the lift and we headed to the designer department. I had expected it to be empty and quiet except for us. But when the lift doors slid back I saw that all of the staff were waiting, waiting just for us.

I have never seen so many beautiful dresses in my life, gowns of all colours and designs all brought out for Imogene to try on one by one.

"A lot of actresses," Imogene told me as she swirled around in a pink princess number, "only use one designer, but I prefer to come here when I'm in London and I need a dress. There's so much beautiful stuff to look at and I guess that this part is still like a fairy tale to me. I used to dream of shopping at Harrods when I was a little girl."

"And me," I said, making everybody laugh for some reason.

At last Imogene came out of the dressing room in a white gown with a hem that seemed to float just above the floor and that was covered in tiny crystals, and shimmered and glittered with every movement.

Farrah and her staff gave a ripple of applause.

"This is the one, Ms Grant," Farrah said. "Stunning.

Perfectly stunning." Imogene smiled politely at Farrah but stood in front of me.

"It really is great, Imogene," Clarice said.

"What do you think, Ruby?" Imogene asked me. "Does it make me look fat?"

I would have laughed if she hadn't been so serious. Imogene Grant, one of the world's most beautiful women, really wanted to know whether or not she looked fat!

"You look beautiful," I told her.

"Great." She smiled at Farrah. "I'll take it," she said, and then she looked at me. "Now it's your turn."

It was late as Imogene's limo pulled up outside our flat.

"What a wonderful evening," my mum said, overwhelmed by our out-of-hours visit to world-famous diamond merchant and jewellers, De Beers. "Thank you so much, Imogene."

"Don't thank me," Imogene said. "I should be thanking you. Going to all this trouble to come and see my movie."

"I can't believe that I'm going to be wearing that many diamonds," I said for about the fourteenth time since we'd got back in the car.

Imogene laughed. "You carry them off wonderfully well. And they looked lovely with that blue silk dress."

"Fifty *thousand* pounds worth of diamonds," I said, still not quite able to believe that *anything* could cost that much, let alone one necklace. "All around *my* neck."

"Yes, well," Imogene said. "Don't forget we have to give them back at the end of the night – and the watch. De Beers will have a whole security team following us around to make sure nothing happens to those diamonds."

"Fifty thousand pounds," I said again.

"Come on," my mum said, putting on her sensible voice again. "You've got lessons in the morning. Bed."

"Bed." I repeated the word and laughed. "I'm never going to be able to sleep!"

"Bet you will," Imogene said, kissing me on the cheek. "See you on set tomorrow."

"I'll never be able to sleep," I told my mum as I sat on the edge of my bed a few minutes later.

"I'll bring you some warm milk," she told me.

But I never got to drink it. I was fast asleep before it came.

The rest of the week seemed to whiz by, one minute in a blur of filming and lessons with Fran Francisco, and then suddenly time would stand still when I had nothing to do but play cards in my Winnebago and listen to Mum going on about Jeremy Fort and what a lovely man he was, and did I think he had a sort of sadness about him, as if he really needed to be looked after? I told her I most certainly did not, and anyway even if he did I was sure that Carenza Slavchenkov cheered him up no end.

At those times it seemed as if Friday, the premiere and seeing Danny again would never come.

I did text and phone Danny a few times during the week, leaving him a message saying that I had something to tell him. But I thought his phone must be broken again because he never replied or called me back. On Thursday night I phoned his house and his mum said he was out again. He'd been out a lot recently and I wondered who with. I asked her to give him a message. I said it was really important, but he hadn't called me back by the time I went to bed. I wasn't worried; I was certain that now I hadn't fallen in love with Sean Rivers everything would be OK with Danny. And anyway, he probably thought that as we would be seeing each other at Nydia's party on Friday, we could talk then.

I had meant to tell Nydia and to explain to her about being late for her party. I meant to, but I didn't for two reasons. First of all, I was worried about telling her; she seemed so fragile at the moment that I worried she might think I didn't want to come, not that I couldn't. So I decided that maybe it would be better not to upset her before the party and to just turn up a bit late with a movie star on my arm, which might make her forget that I had promised to be there from the very beginning of the evening. And secondly, because Sean said it was best not to tell anyone at all that we were still going to Nydia's party.

"But why not?" I asked him. "I mean when I explain it to Mum she'll be fine about it. She'll probably even drive us; we're going home for the weekend anyway."

"Drive us!" Sean exclaimed. "Oh boy, Ruby Parker, you need to work on your sense of adventure," he said.

"My sense of adventure?" I asked him.

"Sure," he said. "It will be much more fun if we *escape*. Besides, my dad would never actually let me go. My only option is to escape."

And even though I am not very good at rebelling, and really don't like to be in trouble, there was something about the daring twinkle in Sean Rivers' eye that made me think it might be fun to turn going to Nydia's party into an escape adventure. After all, I reasoned, it wasn't as if I was doing anything really bad, and I was sure Mum wouldn't be too cross or worried as long as I phoned her as soon as I got there.

Prepare
to be
jealous,
girls!

This week Girly Gossip can exclusively reveal that our most famous reader, Ruby Parker, is having a ball on the set of her first movie, *The Lost Treasure of King Arthur*.

Insiders tell Girly Gossip that Ruby especially enjoys fellow cast member Sean Rivers. Well, who can blame her...? It's a good thing that Ruby's off-screen romance with *Kensington Heights* actor, Danny Harvey, is so solid and that neither one of them seems to be the jealous type, because while Ruby is messing around with Sean (only on set, of course – we wouldn't imply anything else!) Danny has won Girly Gossip's readers' poll for the Best Looking Boy on the Box! Congratulations, Danny and hey, Ruby, if you're missing him while you're shooting your movie you'll find an eight-page pull-out poster spread in next week's edition of *Teen Girl! Magazine!*

"Action!"

Chapter Fourteen

"What do you think?" Mum asked anxiously.

"At last," I said without looking up from my magazine. We had all gone to the same hotel I had my second audition in, the Waldorf, to get ready for the premiere, and Mum and I had our own room and even our own hair and make-up lady, Maxine, who Art had hired just for the evening.

I had been ready for ages, waiting for Mum and Maxine to come out of the bathroom, sitting patiently in my blue dress and diamonds, my hair just left long and natural and with hardly any make-up on at all, despite me trying really hard for some blusher. As I waited, it felt strange to be looking at a magazine full of properly famous people walking up red carpets, knowing that very soon I would be doing the same thing. It felt strange but sort of not real, which meant I probably wasn't nearly as excited as I should have been.

I turned around and looked at Mum. I'd expected her to make an effort but I hadn't expected her to look the way she did.

"Mu-um!" I exclaimed in shock. "What *do* you think you look like?"

Mum's face fell, and I knew instantly that I had hurt her, that somehow she thought that a long green satin dress cut far too low in the chest area and worn with matching high heels she could never walk in in a million years were appropriate for a woman of her age. A woman and a *mother* of her age.

She had gone totally over the top. Mum clasped her hand to her chest and looked down at herself with dismay.

"Do I look terrible, really?" she asked me.

I looked her up and down. Since Dad had left she'd been to a slimming club, so at least she fitted into the dress without too many bulges. And the green colour did suit her complexion and newly auburn hair, which Imogene's hairdresser had dyed for her so that no grey bits showed any more. And at least she wasn't wearing too much make-up; in fact, Maxine had somehow managed to make her face look sort of glowy, if a bit miserable.

"It's not that you don't look nice…" I began, feeling a bit mean and maybe ever so slightly wrong. "It's just that…"

There was a knock at the door. I looked at Mum, who stared at me with an expression of terror.

"Ruby, if I look really terrible I don't want anyone to see me..."

"The door was open," Jeremy Fort said as he entered the room, "so I just thought I'd pop in and see if you needed an escort..." He stopped and looked at my mum standing by the window.

"Janice," he said, his deep voice almost a whisper, "you look stunning."

I watched my mum's face light up as if the sun had just risen inside her head. I looked at Jeremy looking at my mum and thought what an amazing actor he was. He looked at her like he really meant it, like she was the most beautiful woman he had ever seen.

"And you too, Ruby," Jeremy said, still looking at my mother. "Quite wonderful. May I escort you downstairs? They have various limos waiting for us. I wish you were travelling with me, Janice, I'd love to walk you down the red carpet looking like that – but I'm afraid they have a separate car for parents and guardians that will take you to a side entrance."

"Oh, well, of course," Mum said, fluttering her lashes. "I mean, who am I? I'm no one."

"Nonsense," Jeremy said, hooking her arm through

his. "You are Janice Parker and there's only one of you in the whole world." I followed them to the lift, trying to look anywhere except at my mum giggling like an idiot at every word Jeremy said and wishing that he wasn't quite so kind, because really he was only giving my mum false hope.

As we walked out into the chilly evening, Sean was waiting by one of four limos in a pale blue suit and white shirt.

He was wearing sunglasses even though it was dark. On anyone else it would have looked idiotic; on him it looked totally cool. When he saw me, he smiled that famous smile, and for a moment my heart did skip a beat. Because from a distance, in that suit and with that smile, he wasn't my friend Sean, a fifteen-year-old boy bored out of his mind with acting and movie sets and all of that rubbish, he was Sean Rivers, heart-stoppingly-handsome teen-movie star.

Suddenly I realised that Sean was two people – that despite his claims to the contrary he really was a true movie star because he could do what only true stars can: when he needed it, he just turned his starriness on like a thousand-watt light bulb, shining as brightly and as far as a beacon, making it clear as day that he was not just an ordinary person.

For the first time since I had met him, he had turned that light on.

"Steady on," I whispered to myself under my breath. Because even though there was no way I could fall for my friend and fellow actor, Sean, I didn't think it would take very much at all for me to get really silly over the gorgeous star of *The Underdogs*.

"Hey, Ruby Parker!" he called out. "You're in this car with me!"

I tried turning my own star quality on as I walked over to meet him, but when I did it felt more like next door's toddler's nursery night-light in the middle of a power cut. Whatever it was in people like Imogene or Sean that made it impossible for people to stop looking at them – I didn't have it. And that was a fact.

Sean looked at me over the top of his shades as I approached. I braced myself for him to say something romantic and flattering like Jeremy had said to Mum, because I knew if he did my knees would give out and I would need resuscitating.

"You look like a Christmas fairy," he said, winking at me. Not exactly the response I had been expecting, but on the bright side at least I could still walk and breathe. He opened the door and I climbed into the back of the car, discovering that it is far easier said than done in a long tight dress. Sean got in next to me and took off his shades.

"Our own limo," he said. "Awesome! Lisa told me they want to highlight the young actors in our film, get a teen audience interested. So we're on our own, kiddo."

Sean looked around the interior of the car, found and opened the fridge.

"Want a Coke?" he asked me, holding out a bottle. I shook my head.

"Lip gloss," I said by way of explanation, not wanting to tell him I was scared that if I drank too much when I was really nervous I'd end up really needing the loo and would have to run instead of walk up the red carpet to make it to the ladies.

Sean grinned at me. "Can't get used to you all dressed up," he said, peering at me. "Are you in there somewhere, Ruby Parker?"

I let out a breath and laughed. I was relieved to see that in the back of the car he was just Sean again and I didn't fancy him at all. Sean sat back in his seat and sipped his drink.

"So," he said, "I've worked on our escape plan for later. First we do the red carpet thing and then..." His words washed over me as I thought properly for the first time about walking up that red carpet. Suddenly my heart was thundering in my chest and my stomach was clenched as tightly as a fist. In a few minutes I'd be doing the "red carpet thing". I'd be walking up a red carpet and thousands of screaming fans from all around the world would see me stepping out of a limo, look at me and think, "Who *is* that?"

"Ruby Parker?" Sean seemed to be repeating himself. "Are you listening?"

"I'm having a mild panic attack," I said, sounding as if I had inhaled the contents of a helium balloon. Sean laughed.

"Seriously, don't worry," he said. "No one is going to be looking at you."

I opened my mouth to protest but realised that actually he was probably right. No one would be looking at me. It did sort of take the pressure off, even if it was a bit disappointing.

"Sorry," I said, taking a deep breath. "Sometimes I go all over the top about things. So tell me your plan."

Sean peered out of the window. "Too late," he said. "I'll have to tell you later. We're here."

I looked out of the window just as the limo pulled into Leicester Square.

Rows and rows of people were lined up behind

barriers, three or four people deep, and all of them cheering and shouting. Some girls had a banner held up, a bit like the one that the girls outside the café held up for Danny, only much bigger and much better made.

SEAN RIVERS WILL YOU MARRY US?

"Blimey," I said.

"I know," Sean said, chuckling. "Blimey." He peered out of the tinted window at the crowds. "Imogene will go in first with the other actors from *Lizzie Bennet* – you know that English guy that's in all of your movies? The one with the floppy hair and the stupid voice?"

"Oh, him," I said.

"Exactly," Sean said. "And some other grand British thespian, oh, you know, what's her name? The one that's a lady, or a duchess or something?"

"Dame Judi," I said, biting my lip at the thought of one of my all-time heroines and forgetting completely about my lip gloss.

"That's her," Sean said. "Then it'll be Harry, Art and Jeremy. And then us."

Sean rolled down the window a crack and we listened as the cheers grew. From where we were parked we couldn't see the length of the red carpet, but we knew who was on it by the names the fans called out as they went by.

"Imogene always talks to as many fans as she can," Sean said. "So we'll be here ages while people get her to pose for photos and phone up their grannies and things like that." He wasn't wrong. It seemed like an eternity that we sat in the back of that limo, listening to the crowds cheering as I chewed every last bit of lip gloss off my mouth and dug my short nails into my palms.

And then suddenly the limo door opened and the noise was magnified by about a hundred million times.

Lisa Wells was there telling us we had to get out of the car. As I stepped out she looked me up and down and then, pulling a tube of lip gloss out of her bag, she reapplied some to my mouth.

"Don't look so scared, Ruby," she told me. "You look great. Off you go."

"Off I go where?" I asked her, but before I knew it Lisa's team of publicists had swept me away from the safety of the shelter that standing in Sean's shadow provided and they propelled me forward the last few metres until I was suddenly all alone.

All alone at the end of the red carpet.

It seemed to me as if everyone and everything fell silent. The crowd, the press, the traffic, the pigeons – they were all quiet – as if God had pressed the mute button on his cosmic remote control. The whole world was silent, frozen still and waiting for me. Waiting for me to move.

I tried to but I couldn't. Every time I tried it felt as if I was glued to the spot. I tried to turn on some star quality, like Sean did. And when that didn't work I tried to just smile my average smile, but even then nothing happened. I was like a rabbit caught in the headlights of an oncoming juggernaut. All I could do was stand there and stare at it getting ready to run me down.

Somewhere in the tiny part of my brain that was still working I realised that the moment I had dreamed about for so long was going horribly wrong. That tiny part of me knew that my first – and at this rate quite possibly my last ever – red-carpet experience was a disaster, and that I'd be rooted to that tiny patch of red carpet for ever and ever like one of those dreadful mime statues you see hanging around Covent Garden.

"Hey, Ruby Parker," Sean's friendly voice whispered in my ear. "I'm glad you waited for me. I could do with someone to hold my hand."

And in that moment it was just like when Prince Charming wakes up Sleeping Beauty with a single kiss. The sound of Sean's voice in my ear had exactly the same effect, and before I knew it the deafening noise of the crowd rushed in all around me and I was back in the world again. Sean held tightly on to my hand and I knew that as long as he did I could make it from where we were standing to the other end of the red carpet in one piece.

"Let's knock 'em dead," Sean said, switching on his starriness, and we stepped out into the glare of the lights and glitter of flashbulbs, hand in hand, side by side.

"Sean! Sean!" Hundreds of reporters called Sean's name as we made our way towards the entrance of the cinema. Sean squeezed my hand and led me to the first in a row of microphones, each carrying a badge marked with a different TV station or show logo.

"Sean." The first reporter, Tilly James from *Celebrity Central*, grabbed Sean's arm. I had done an interview with her once but she didn't even glance at me. "Great to see you in London, but tell us, why are you here supporting Imogene Grant's new film?"

"Well," Sean told Tilly, with a relaxed smile, "I'm working on a new film along with Imogene, Jeremy Fort and Ruby Parker here." Sean nodded at me but Tilly didn't take her eyes off his face. "It's an action adventure called *The Lost Treasure of King Arthur* and we're shooting it right now at the Elm Tree Studios. Imogene invited us along tonight, and you know I never like to miss a party!"

"And what do you think of London?" Tilly asked Sean.

"I *love* London, I love this country – especially the weather!" Sean said, laughing as a fine cold drizzle started at that moment. The reporter turned to the camera.

"That was Sean Rivers talking exclusively to *Celebrity Central*, exclusively on…"

We moved down the line from reporter to reporter, me standing behind Sean and waiting as he answered almost exactly the same question from each reporter with almost exactly the same answer and the same incredible smile.

He must have repeated himself at least ten times as gradually the haven of the cinema doors grew closer. It was just as I thought we were nearly there that I realised we still had one last thing to do.

Pose for the paparazzi – the ruthless pack of press photographers that followed celebrities everywhere they went and would stop at nothing to get a good picture.

Sean led me out into the middle of the red carpet, and it seemed as if the crowd must only have been made up of girls like me because they erupted in a frenzied scream. Sean waved at them and blew them kisses, without letting go of my hand. In fact, holding it so tightly that I wondered if he hadn't been joking after all when he said he needed someone's hand to hold.

Finally we walked past the bank of press photographers, their flashes ignited like a firework display. I'd seen soap actors and actresses doing this thousands of times – stop for the paparazzi, knowing exactly how to stand and exactly where to smile. I'd even done it myself once or twice on my way into soap awards, not that my photos ever appeared in any papers.

But now I was here, living my dream, all I wanted to do was to stand as far behind Sean as I could and wait for it to be over.

"So who's your girlfriend?" one of the photo-graphers called out. Sean laughed and pulled me forward so that I was standing, blinking in the full glare of the cameras.

"Don't you know?" he shouted back. "This is Ruby Parker! From *Kensington Heights*! She's in my new movie too. Keep an eye out for Ruby; she's the next big thing."

"Sorry, Ruby," one photographer called. "Didn't recognise you there in a posh frock."

"Give us a smile, Ruby," another one called. So I did, and it didn't feel too bad. I smiled again and the click of flashes went off every time that I did. By the third or fourth smile I was getting quite into it.

But I wasn't prepared for what happened next.

"Give her a kiss then, Sean," a third one shouted, and before I knew it, Sean Rivers did kiss me. And it wasn't Sean my friend, it was THE Sean Rivers. Kissing ME, Ruby Parker. In front of all those people.

It wasn't a romantic kiss or anything like that. Sean just put his hand on my waist and turned me towards him before landing a quick peck on my lips – it was over in less than a second. But in that second a thousand TV and photographic cameras were pointed at us, all of them capturing that moment and freezing it into an everlasting kiss.

"Oh dear," I said to Sean, who was giving the crowd one last wave. "What if they print a photo of us kissing?"

"Does it matter?" Sean said, and I realised that in our whole week together I hadn't talked about Danny once, and he didn't know I had a boyfriend who might get the wrong idea about those pictures. "Anyway," Sean continued, "they're not going to put you and me in the papers, Ruby, not when they've got Imogene Grant to put there. Don't worry about it; it doesn't mean anything."

Just then the rain really started to come down and at last Sean and I ran inside where Lisa was waiting for us.

"Good job, guys," Lisa said. "That kiss was very cute. I think you really drummed up some interest in our film. Now follow me and I'll show you the way to the party."

"Don't we get to see the film?" I asked her, still half-blinded by the flash bulbs and reeling from the intensity of the red-carpet experience.

"Don't be dumb," Sean said. "No one who's anyone ever sees the film at these things. We have our own so-called VIP party to go to, although they usually let in anyone who's ever been famous for fifteen minutes. And then later the masses – competition winners and corporate groups who have seen the film – come in and try and catch a glimpse of us beyond the ropes. That's how it works."

"Oh," I said, a little disappointed. "I really wanted to see the film."

"Well, you'll have to go another day, Ruby," Sean told me as he bent his head close to mine. "Cos all we're doing today is showing our faces at the party. We make our excuses and then we break out, head off to your friend's crib and party hard."

"I did tell you it's just pizzas and maybe a DVD, didn't I?" I asked him. "It won't be a party, party. It's just Nydia, her family, Anne-Marie and my boyfriend Danny, he will be there. It won't be an actual party."

"Ruby Parker," Sean said, winking at me, "don't you know by now – *everything's* a party when I'm involved."

"Action!"

Chapter Fifteen

When we walked into the roped-off VIP part of the premiere party, my mum and Sean's dad were waiting for us. Sean's dad had this huge grin plastered on his face which reminded me of Sean's smile, only without any of the warmth and, well, the happiness that really should go with huge smiles.

"Darling!" Mum said, her cheeks flushed. "You were wonderful. Really great!"

"Was I?" I said – wondering how she knew.

"Oh, yes, we saw you on the TV." She gestured at one of the many screens that were positioned around the room. "It was live on the London evening news."

"Was it?" I asked her uneasily, wondering if Danny and Nydia had been watching the news while they were still waiting for me to turn up. I looked at my borrowed diamond-encrusted watch that was worth fifteen thousand pounds. It said that I was now an hour and forty minutes late for Nydia's party. I didn't have any money or my phone on me, so I couldn't ring them and tell them I was planning to come. And now there was every chance they would have seen me and Sean on the evening news and would be thinking I had forgotten all about them completely. And I suppose, in a way, I sort of had. I sort of wanted to.

I looked around at the party thronged with celebrities from lists A to Z. Sean was right, they seemed to have let most of the UK's celebrities in, all looking for even a sniff of publicity. As I wondered how Sean and I would ever break out of this crowd, I realised that my plan not to tell Nydia that I would be late wasn't just because I didn't want to upset her, it was because even though it meant letting a friend down, I had wanted to be at this premiere tonight and I thought that Nydia wouldn't have understood. And even though I left messages for Danny asking him to call me, I could have easily texted him and told him what was happening, but I didn't.

I didn't because deep down I wanted to keep this new life, this new and exciting life where I was someone so different and important, far, far away from my old life where I was just Ruby Parker, mid-to-low-popularity-ranking ex-soap schoolgirl actress who was always getting picked second from last for netball. I had thought I could keep my new life and my old separate and still have both, being a different version of Ruby Parker in each part. I suppose the reason I wanted to keep them apart was because I was afraid of the way I was changing and afraid that my friends wouldn't like it.

Being a part of *The Lost Treasure of King Arthur* had made me see myself differently, had made me have more confidence in my acting and more confidence in myself. And even when I walked down the red carpet as terrified as a person could be, now that I had done it, I had changed a little bit more. Because I knew that if I had the chance to do it again, I would be better at it.

But the sick and guilty feeling I had in the pit of my stomach at the thought of seeing Nydia, Danny and Anne-Marie watching me on TV, and knowing that I hadn't exactly lied to them but hadn't exactly told them the truth, made me realise the truth: that this life, the glamorous life, wasn't my *real* life, and that I didn't want to throw away my old friends so easily for something that would be over all too soon and might never come back.

I knew I had to get to Nydia's as soon as possible.

I turned to look at Sean, who was in a very close and quiet conversation with his father. I couldn't hear what they were saying, but it looked to me as if they were arguing about something. Or rather, Sean's father was arguing, and Sean, head bowed, face closed, was listening as if his dad's words were as heavy and hard as hail stones.

I hovered for a moment longer, hoping that Sean would look up and see me, but he didn't. It was no good; I decided I would just have to tell Mum that I needed to go to Nydia's and ask her to lend me the money for a taxi. After all, Sean's idea to keep it all one big secret seemed rather silly now.

I turned back to talk to Mum but she had gone, drifted off amidst the glittering cloud of satin and silk created by celebrities dressed for a big night out. I could just see the back of her bobbing and nodding as she cornered poor Jeremy Fort again.

Looking back at Sean, I could see he was still entangled in conversation with his father. Pat Rivers' face looked so deadly that I was certain Sean's plans to accompany me to Nydia's party were officially over. I wanted to stay close to Sean and make sure that he was OK but I also needed to get to Nydia's and see her and Danny, so I decided to make my way towards Mum.

"Ruby, darling!" A familiar voice sounded like a siren in my ear. And I heard the "mwah! mwah!" of a kiss delivered about a centimetre away from each cheek.

I made myself smile at Brett Summers, who officially

confirmed that this was a VIP party that anyone could get into.

"How lovely to see you, darling!" Brett gushed as if she hadn't tried to get me fired from *Kensington Heights* and finish my acting career before it had even begun. "And you look wonderful! I can't believe how you have changed since I saw you last – my little girl all grown up! A real little lady and working on a movie now with Imogene Grant!" It seemed as if Brett couldn't finish a sentence without a verbal exclamation mark tagged on the end. I nodded and wondered how quickly I could escape her clutches.

"Mmmm," I said.

"Of course, I knew her when she was *no one*, darling!" Brett fluttered her false lashes at me. "I don't suppose she remembers me, does she? Does she ever talk about me?"

I took a step back from Brett, who seemed to be slightly lopsided and holding a glass of champagne in one hand at an angle that would have caused it to spill if it still had any champagne left in it.

"Um... not really, no," I said. Brett's painted-on smile turned sour for a moment and I think she would have frowned if her forehead hadn't been frozen by some chemical cosmetic procedure.

"Well, anyway, I'm so glad I saw you because, well, I've always thought that I had a hand in making you what you are today, and I feel as if really I passed the torch on to you – the new generation." I tried not to laugh out loud. "But I want you to know, Ruby, that now it's up to you to help me, your mentor. I've had no luck since I was… since I left the show. So I was wondering if you could talk to Mr Dubrovnik for me about finding me a part in your film?" I wanted to say she'd be perfect for the part of the mummified killer zombie-witch and wouldn't even need make-up, but I didn't because I couldn't quite bring myself to be that rude. And besides, Brett when she's angry is far scarier than a mummified killer zombie-witch.

"I don't think that I…" I had begun when Sean appeared at my side.

"Excuse me," Sean said. I could see with one glance at his tense white face that he was very angry and upset. "I'm sorry to interrupt," Sean said, his voice polite but tight, "but Ruby and I have an engagement we have to get to, right, Ruby?"

"Right," I said to Sean. I flashed my fakest smile at Brett. "Must dash! Cheerio!"

"Oh!" Brett looked affronted. "Well, Ruby, if you could just talk to… Ruby!"

But I was already following Sean as he weaved in and out of the partygoers, keeping his head down as he went, avoiding any chance of having to stop and make small talk. I glanced over my shoulder at Mum, who was still talking to Jeremy. I saw her put her hand on his shoulder and toss her red hair as she laughed. A moment ago I had wanted to tell her that I was leaving but now suddenly I did not.

If she was happy to go off and make a fool of herself over Jeremy without even wondering where I was then let her find out later that I've gone. Suddenly I didn't care if she worried. I wanted her to; I wanted her to think about something else apart from Jeremy Fort for five seconds.

We left the noise and the heat of the party, turning into a long corridor as I rushed after Sean who was stalking towards the back of the building.

"Sean!" I called after him. "Are you OK?"

"I'm fine," he said, which was obviously a lie.

"Where are we going?" I asked him, hitching my blue silk skirt up a little further so that I could lengthen my steps and catch him up. "What's the plan?"

Sean stopped dead and I ran into the back of him. He turned around and helped me steady myself before taking a deep breath and trying to find his smile, but it seemed only just about there.

"I'm sorry, Ruby Parker," he said, his voice low. "It's

just my dad. He just doesn't get that I'm still only a kid, you know? The minute I got to the party, the second after we walked the red carpet, he's laying into me about kissing you – that stupid little kiss that didn't mean a thing. All he cares about is that I might upset my fans, who might not buy my merchandise or see my movies any more because they think you're my girlfriend. Well, I tell you what – I wish they wouldn't, because then I'd be out of a job! And then he's telling me about another project he's agreed for me and another one after that." Sean ran his fingers through his hair. "Ruby, I've got the next three years of my life planned out for me already, and during those three years between working and studying not once is there any time just for me to be... me."

Sean looked quickly at his feet and I got the feeling that he was trying not to cry.

"But you do want to be an actor, don't you?" I asked him in wonder, because his life sounded just about perfect to me. Sean dug his hand into his trouser pockets and shook his head without looking up.

"You know what?" he said, finally looking me in the eye. "I'd rather stay home and read a book, or play football in the park with my friends. I'd rather do my homework in *one* place, go to school in *one* place and live in *one* place. I'd like to have a dog. I'd like to make friends I could keep longer than three months. I'd like to meet a girl to take to the prom and know guys to hang out with while she's dancing. I didn't choose this life, Ruby, it chose me. And now it feels like it's... smothering me or... Oh, I don't know what I'm talking about." I reached out and held his hand.

"Then just leave it, Sean, just stop," I said. Sean shrugged and chewed his lip.

"That's just it," he said. "I can't. Dad won't let me. I'm making him richer than he ever dreamed he could be. And it's like he keeps saying, I've got the family to think of. The family needs me to keep working. Well, I'm an only kid and I don't see my mom any more so he *is* my family." I hesitated to ask my next question as I looked at Sean struggling to keep his anger and hurt under control.

"Why don't you see your mum?" I asked him eventually. "Can't you tell her how unhappy you are and tell her to come and get you?" From the look on Sean's face I had a sudden terrible feeling. "Oh, Sean," I whispered. "Is she dead?"

Sean surprised me by laughing, a mirthless, unhappy bark of a laugh.

"Worse than dead," he said bitterly. "She doesn't want to know me. Hasn't done since her and Dad divorced. I don't know exactly how it happened, I was still pretty young at the time, but it was soon after I got famous during that commercial that they broke up. I woke up one night and Dad was packing all my stuff into a bag. He said we were going on vacation. I didn't realise until the next day that we had gone without Mom." I watched Sean's gaze as he seemed to focus on a distant memory. "They used to scream and argue but I can't really remember why, only that one minute Mom wanted and loved me and the next minute she was gone. There was this big court thing – I remember having to tell a social worker or someone that I wanted to live with my dad. I mean what else could I say? I knew she didn't want me. She couldn't have because she didn't try and keep me, she didn't fight for me."

Sean's voice strained under the weight of emotions he was feeling and I didn't know what to say, so I said nothing. We stood for a second or two longer in the corridor and I watched Sean repeat a routine I was beginning to feel he had performed more than once. He seemed to doggedly put himself back together piece by piece until at last he lifted his chin, looked me in the face and turned on his smile at full brightness.

"Let's forget about all that," he said as if we had just had a normal conversation. "Come on, Ms Parker – it's getting late and we've got a party to get to!"

Somehow I knew that forcing Sean to talk more wouldn't help him, and besides, I didn't think I would have anything helpful to say to him. Of all the things that had happened in my life, the sad things and difficult things, at least I knew that both of my parents loved me and supported me. I had no idea what to say to someone who seemed to be frightened of one parent and never saw the other one. So I followed Sean to the back of the building down to the lower levels and out through a fire exit. It was amazingly easy to run away. Not one person stopped us; the people that passed didn't even look at us. When the alarm went off on the fire exit door, people just walked past as if nothing had happened, as if it wasn't unusual for two teenagers in evening dress, one of whom was world famous, to be wandering about the back entrance of the Odeon Leicester Square. And maybe in London it wasn't.

We came out at the back of the cinema in a narrow alley that runs along the edge of China Town, and while we had been inside it had got dark and the rain had stopped, leaving black puddles in the road reflecting the glare of the brightly coloured lights back up at the night. I breathed in the delicious smell of crispy duck and my tummy rumbled.

"Taxi!" Sean hailed a black cab that was just passing the bottom of the alley.

"You got any money?" he asked me.

"Nope," I said as we climbed in. Sean grinned at me and produced a crocodile-skin wallet from his jacket pocket.

"Good job I 'borrowed' Daddy's wallet then, isn't it?" he said.

I decided that there was no point in saying anything at all and that we were probably in so much trouble already that we couldn't get into any more. I gave the driver Nydia's address. As we sped off out of the city centre I paused and looked out of the back window. I had no idea how angry or worried Mum was going to be when she found out I had gone, and no idea how angry and annoyed my friends were going to be when we got to Nydia's house.

"Oh, well," I said, more or less to myself, "at least I'm being rebellious at last."

But when I thought that Sean and I couldn't get into any more trouble – well – I was seriously wrong about that.

"Action!"

Chapter Sixteen

"Hello, hello," I said breezily to Nydia. "Sorry we're late. We brought some food! I held up a bag of crisps and chocolate that Sean and I had bought at the corner shop with his dad's money.

"I love this town," Sean had said to me as we left the shop. "No one cares who you are. You go into a shop and buy snacks with a girl in a blue ball gown and no one even raises an eyebrow." I shrugged, feeling my nerves grow as we approached Nydia's house.

"Well, Mr Memhet's known me since I was a baby," I said. "And he's probably never heard of you."

"Awesome," Sean had said, and he really meant it.

Now, as we stood on Nydia's doorstep, she looked from me to Sean and her eyes widened.

"Sean Rivers!" she squeaked. I breathed out a sigh of relief; it looked as if she might be so impressed by Sean that she'd forget to be cross with me for being really late.

"Hey, pleased to meet you," Sean said, reaching out and shaking Nydia's hand. "I hope you don't mind me crashing your party, but it's so good to get out of 'movie world' for a little while and hang with some real people, you know?" Sean smiled at Nydia who seemed frozen to the spot.

"Shall we go in?" Sean suggested, which reanimated Nydia.

"Yes, yes, of course," she said, stepping back to let him by. "Ruby did tell you, didn't she, that it's not a party, party? It *was* a family thing with a few friends, to celebrate because I've got a part in a TV show…"

"Cool," Sean said. "What part are you playing?"

"It's not very important really," Nydia said quickly. "But anyway, Mum and Dad are out, giving lifts home to my grannies, and my brothers are out with their mates. In fact, it wasn't much of a party before you got here, and now…" Nydia looked anxious, but Sean beamed at her.

"Well, it's a good job I've arrived then, isn't it?" he said. "Let's get this party started." I flashed a grin at Nydia but she stared back still looking as if she had just witnessed first-hand a real-life alien encounter.

"Sean Rivers!" Anne-Marie appeared in the door. For a moment she was as silly and as giggly as a girl confronted with her dream boyfriend could be, and then she seemed to collect herself and transformed before our eyes into her old cool blonde self.

"We saw you on the news, Rube," she said, arching an eyebrow. "We thought you'd ditched us for Sean, but then nobody could blame you." Anne-Marie stared intensely at Sean as if he were the waxwork dummy of himself that had just gone on show at Madame Tussauds.

This might have been embarrassing and uncomfortable for Sean Rivers except that he was staring back at Anne-Marie in exactly the same way, and she didn't even have a waxwork dummy.

"Um, hi," Sean said, and suddenly all his smooth confidence seem to evaporate. He looked just like a normal fifteen-year-old boy again, not that I got to hang out with that many fifteen-year-old boys. Any actually. Apart from Sean.

I looked at Nydia, who was rolling her eyes, and remembered that Sean was her crush too.

"Hello," Anne-Marie said, holding out her hand. "I'm Anne-Marie Chance. I go to school with Ruby. Of course I know who you are." She smiled and Sean's cheeks flushed a deep red. "Come into the living room and have some cold pizza." Anne-Marie made the invitation sound impossible to resist. "It's not much of a party really but I bet it's sometimes nice for a big movie star like you to hang out with some real people…"

I watched, impressed, as Anne-Marie led Sean into Nydia's living room.

"That girl is amazing," I said to Nydia. "You'd think she ran into a movie-star heart-throb that she had a huge crush on and a shrine made out of posters to in her bedroom every day of the week."

"Yes," Nydia said, her voice cold. "You would."

I looked at her. She clearly hadn't forgotten to be angry with me at all.

"Nydia, I'm sorry I was late," I began, hoping to get past her being cross with me as quickly as possible so that I could talk to Danny about that kiss. "But I had to go to the premiere. Art said I did and I was going to phone and tell you but…"

"You didn't," she said.

"No, I didn't because, well…" I struggled to find a way to say what I meant. "Look, Nydia, you've been really strange recently, ever since I got the part of Polly Harris and, well, it's just not easy to talk to you any more…"

"What, not like your new film-star friends?" Nydia said, nodding towards the living room where Sean and Anne-Marie had put on some loud music.

"I thought you'd be glad I brought Sean," I said. "I thought you'd like to meet him."

"Well, I would have," Nydia said. "But now Anne-Marie's got her claws into him I don't expect he'll have time to talk to me." Nydia crossed her arms.

I held out the bag of crisps and chocolate. "I brought you food?" I offered.

Nydia snatched the bag and threw it on the floor.

"You just don't get it, do you?" she yelled at me.

I stared at the contents of the bag which were scattered across the floor.

"I don't," I said. "I know I was a bit, OK – very – late, and I know it was stupid not to just ring you and tell you why. I don't know why I didn't. I'm sorry for that, I really am." I looked at her face, which was so hard and cold and not like the old smiling Nydia at all. "But even though I've told you I'm sorry, you're still angry with me," I said, and then I realised something. "You were angry with me before you even knew I was going to be late, weren't you? You would still have been like this If I had turned up three days early!" I shook my head in confusion. "What have I done so wrong, Nydia?"

"Nothing. You haven't done anything wrong. *You* never do," Nydia said. "Everything always goes right for you. You mess up an audition so badly that you are actually sick and you still get the part! You never had to worry about fees or about whether you'd get a new scholarship each year. And I stuck by you, kept on being your stupid fat friend even when no one else could stand you – always moaning about being famous and how hard it was, when the rest of us were wishing we had even half of the chances you've had." I opened my mouth and shut it again.

It had never occurred to me that I might be *especially* lucky; I had always thought that people like Anne-Marie, with the money, the looks and the swimming pool, were the lucky ones. But I supposed out of all of the children at the academy, maybe I *was* the one to be envied. I was the one who was doing what all of us dreamed about. But even so, I had never imagined that Nydia, my nearly twin, could be jealous of me. Just as she knew I would never be jealous of her. And then I realised – maybe that was the problem.

"Who helped you when you had to do that kissing scene with Justin on *Kensington Heights* in the summer? And you got all panicky because you'd never kissed anyone." Nydia narrowed her eyes at me. "Me, the same silly old Nydia, always there for you, always thinking about you – well, who thinks about me?"

"I do," I said. "I do, honestly, all the time."

"Like you were tonight?" she said.

"I'm here now, aren't I?" I pleaded, hoping that at any moment her face would be transformed by one of her smiles. "Please don't be angry any more, Nyds. Let's make up. You know you're a brilliant friend – the best."

"I am," Nydia said. "Are you?"

"I…" I suddenly felt very stupid in my blue satin dress and diamonds in Nydia's hallway. My shoulders drooped and I knew that whatever I said next would not be the right thing. "I thought I was."

"You shouldn't have got that part," Nydia said. "Everybody else who auditioned for it deserved it more than you. It's not fair; you only got it because of who you are."

"That's not true," I protested, starting to feel quite angry myself.

"And the one night when you know how much I really wanted you to be around – where are you? On TV kissing somebody else in front of Danny."

"Nydia!" I snapped at her. "I'm here now, aren't I? And anyway, that kiss was just for the camera. Danny won't mind…" I stopped talking and looked at the living-room door behind which Danny would be waiting. I really wanted to see him.

"Won't he?" Nydia said. I took a step closer to my old friend.

"Nydia, please," I said, making a last attempt to stop this going too far. "Let's not fall out. We don't really have anything to fall out about, do we? I'm sorry if you think I shouldn't have got the part, but I did get it. And I think I'm doing a pretty good job of it. And if it was the other way round, if it had been you, I would have been so pleased for you, Nydia."

Nydia kicked a family-size pack of Maltesers in my direction.

"Yes, but it's never *me*, is it, Ruby?" she said. "It's always, always *you*."

She ran up the stairs and after a few moments I heard her door slam shut.

For the first time in our friendship I found that I didn't know how to talk to her. I didn't know what to say that would stop her being angry with me, just for being me.

I bent down and scooped up the food that lay scattered across the hall and bundled it back into the carrier bag. If it had just been me and Nydia and I hadn't been wearing a long blue satin dress and diamonds, I would have left then, gone home, put my pyjamas on and gone to bed. But Danny was sitting waiting for me in the other room and, although I had been hoping during my argument with Nydia that he would come out and rescue me, he hadn't, and I still needed to talk to him.

I pushed open the living-room door and saw that Anne-Marie and Sean had pushed Mrs Assimin's coffee table to one side of the room and were dancing in front of the gas fire. Danny was sitting on the sofa looking out of the patio doors and into the garden.

"Hello, Danny," I said. When he heard my voice he stood up and smiled at me.

"Wow!" he said. "You look amazing. Better than on the telly."

I smiled back at him. Danny was the first person to say anything about the way I looked, and whether or not the dress and diamonds made any difference at all to plain old Ruby Parker, he was the only person that really even noticed *me* at all the whole evening.

"I tried to call you this week," I said, suddenly wishing I had some pockets to put my stupid hands in. As if reading my mind Danny nodded and stuffed his hands in his pockets. Usually about five seconds after meeting each other we are holding hands. Now it felt as if doing something so simple and easy seemed impossible.

"I know," he said with a shrug.

I glanced round at where Anne-Marie and Sean were twisting quite inappropriately to an American rock band that one of Nydia's brothers was into, laughing their heads off as they danced.

"You met Sean then?" I asked him. Danny nodded.

"He said hi. He didn't seem that interested in me."

I smiled. "That's Anne-Marie for you," I said. "She's got hypnotic powers."

Danny and I stood looking at each other by the sofa, and it felt that we were about a kilometre apart instead of just a few centimetres, and Danny might as well have been a tiny spot on a far horizon, because even as I stood right in front of him I couldn't tell what he was thinking or feeling.

"I can't believe you didn't tell me you were going to a premiere," Danny said finally. "Like, I mean, I saw you on the *news*, Rube."

"I tried to phone," I repeated. "I phoned you and texted you and left messages with your mum but you didn't call me back." Danny glanced at the carpet and then back at me.

"I know," he said. "I'm sorry – I just thought that, well – I didn't know if you wanted me to."

"Why not?" I was amazed.

"Well, I thought that maybe you were changing your mind about... well, me, I suppose," Danny half-mumbled, suddenly not able to look me in the eye.

I stared at him. "What?" I asked him. "But why?"

"Hey, Ruby Parker," Sean yelled over the music. "Come and dance." I smiled at Sean but shook my head.

"I'm talking to Danny – this is Danny, my *boyfriend*." I said the last word with as much emphasis as I could and looked hard at Danny, who went to the patio door and opened it.

"Can we talk outside?" he asked me, shooting a narrow look at Sean. "I can't hear myself in here."

I nodded and followed him.

The evening was cold and damp and as soon as I stepped outside I felt the goose bumps rising on my hands. Danny slid his denim jacket off and draped it around my shoulders.

"Thank you," I said, wishing he wasn't being so formal, wishing that he'd just put his arms around me and hug me like he used to.

"So what's the great Sean Rivers like then?" Danny asked me, nodding back at Sean and Anne-Marie, who we could see through the patio doors had flopped down on to the sofa and were talking and laughing as if they'd known each other for ever.

"He's really great," I said warmly, and then seeing the shadows on Danny's face added, "but he's just a really good friend."

"Yeah, I could tell that by the way you were kissing him," Danny said darkly.

"Oh, that," I said. I felt my tummy churn with so many emotions I couldn't tell what I was feeling. Anger was the one that surfaced first. All I had done was to come around to spend some time with my friends and my boyfriend and so far all I got was attacked for doing absolutely nothing wrong. "It was just a peck, Danny – hardly anything – and it was just Sean messing around for the cameras. I didn't even know he was going to do it until he did it." I tried to sound jokey. "I mean it was over in a nanosecond."

"You looked like you enjoyed it," Danny started. And it was then that I really lost my temper.

"Oh, Danny!" I raised my voice in frustration. "It was a stupid five-second kiss, it's not a big deal! This is so silly! It's like, it's like a stupid scene from *Kensington Heights*!"

Danny's face clouded over dangerously.

"Oh, so now you're a movie star you think *Kensington Heights* is stupid, do you?" he said sulkily.

"Danny!" I said in exasperation. "*You* think *Kensington Heights* is stupid – you've said it enough times! And anyway – you *know* what I mean."

"I thought I did," Danny said. "But you're not you any more, Rube. You've changed."

"Can't I change?" I asked him. "*You've* changed. You've changed a lot since you started on *Kensington Heights*, topping readers' polls in magazines – and I'm not getting all freaked out."

"You freaked out about my fan letters," Danny reminded me.

"For about five seconds," I admitted. "And then I realised I was being a total moron, like someone else I could mention is being right now." I challenged Danny with a stare, but as I watched him his shoulders relaxed and all of the tense lines seemed to drain out of his body.

"I'm sorry," he said with a small smile. "I'm so stupid sometimes."

"Oh, Danny," I said, venturing a smile back.

But before I could run up to him and hug him he added, "Just as long as that Sean bloke knows that you belong to me."

I felt the heat in my cheeks sharply against the cold air as I suddenly grew tired of everyone being angry with me, and got angry myself.

"Danny, I don't *belong* to anyone!" I found myself shouting at him.

Danny and I stared at each other for a long moment.

"Right," Danny said stiffly. "So what are you saying then? That you don't want to go out with me any more too, now that I'm not good enough for you?"

And what I wanted to say was, "Of course I want to go out with you, you idiot, just as long as you stop being so silly and jealous and we can go back to having fun again." But I was so tired, so angry and annoyed at Danny for somehow managing to create this whole drama out of nothing at all, and at myself for not being able to make him see sense, that I hesitated. I wondered if I really did want to be with him, if being with him meant going through all of this.

First one second, and then two, three, four, five slipped by. It was about four seconds too long for Danny to wait.

"Fine," he said, starting back towards the house. "Fine. Bye then."

"Danny!" I called after him. "You didn't let me speak!"

Danny stopped at the patio doors and looked round at me.

"You didn't have to," he said. "It's obvious how you feel."

"But, Danny, I was just..." Danny swung the door shut behind him and left me shivering in the garden for a moment. I was furious with him for acting like an idiot, but I couldn't believe that we had ended. Over nothing.

I couldn't leave it that way, I just couldn't.

I ran into the house leaving the patio door swinging open behind me. I ran into the hallway where the door had just slammed shut as Danny left, and I ran out of the front door. And I would have caught up with Danny, and maybe would have been able to make him see what he was doing, and maybe might have made everything all right again.

Except that was when I got arrested.

TEEN STAR SWEETHEARTS FLEE PREMIERE WITH PRICELESS DIAMONDS!

Last night American teen sensation Sean Rivers and ex-*Kensington Heights* star Ruby Parker almost pulled off one of the greatest diamond heists the country has ever seen – and all by accident!

Young Love?

The couple attended the premiere of Imogene Grant's new film *Lizzie Bennet* last night, walking down the red carpet hand in hand. Sean broke the hearts of millions of his fans when he kissed Ruby in front of the world's press (photo, bottom right).

Hands

Sean clearly displayed his passion for Ruby as they embraced each other as if in a world of their own. Fifteen-year-old Sean is renowned for leaving a string of celebrity starlets in his wake. And he's certainly got his hands on some top British totty in talented teen Ruby.

Flight

It's unclear what happened next, but Sean Rivers was seen having a heated discussion with his father and manager Patrick Rivers. Close personal friends of Sean say that Patrick Rivers was telling him to stay away from British protégée Ruby Parker, as she would ruin his heart-throb image. Determined to be together the passionate pair left the party in secret.

Alarm

The love-struck youngsters had been gone for nearly an hour before people started to miss them. Ruby's mother/manager Janice Parker was said to be beside herself with worry and feared kidnapping. The police were called in and that's when they realised Ruby was still wearing nearly sixty-five thousand pounds worth of jewellery borrowed from world-famous diamond importers and jewellers De Beers. Insiders feared the pair planned to elope to parts of the US where underage marriage is still legal.

Wild Party

Luckily, Oscar-winning movie mogul Art Dubrovnik, who is directing the teen stars in his new project *The Lost Treasure of King Arthur*, remembered that Ruby had promised to visit a friend's party that evening in Highgate. Police rushed to the scene and found Ruby and Sean partying with Ruby's friends, unaware of the panic they had caused. Ruby and Sean were then escorted back to

De Beers, where they handed over the jewellery and, inside sources say, "were given a good talking to".

Embarrassed

When asked, upon returning to the five-star Central London hotel they were staying in, what had been going through their minds as they left the party, Ruby said, "Nothing really. I hadn't even remembered I was wearing the De Beers diamonds – I really am ever so sorry!" When asked the same question, Sean Rivers put his arm around Ruby's shoulder and told us with a wink, "We just needed some time alone!"

Attention

Now Ruby Parker can be assured that the world will be focused on the young British girl who seems to have caught heart-throb Sean Rivers. What can be next for Ruby Parker?

Chapter Seventeen

"But none of that is true!" I looked at the morning paper in dismay. Mum clattered a plate of toast on to the table and sat opposite me, thudding into her chair. "Hardly any of it," I added nervously. Mum had jumped right to the front of the long queue of people who weren't very happy with me.

I had hoped I could have got away with it. Last night when Mum first saw me after we got back, all she did was cry and laugh at the same time. She ran up to me and grabbed me and kissed me all over my face and hugged me so tightly I thought my ribs would break. Even Dad was there too and the three of us hugged each other for a long time, and I did think to myself that actually maybe accidentally stealing all those diamonds wasn't such a bad thing – it made us a family again, if only for a little while.

Mum had said she wanted to be at home – not at our flat but at our real home – and so did I, so Dad drove us back to our house, while Mum and I sat in the back of his car holding hands. When we got in, Everest was there sitting in the hallway as if he knew we were coming. As we opened the door he even hauled himself off his fat belly and lurched towards us meowing a greeting.

"I think next door are feeding him too much," Mum said.

"Yes, but which next door?" Dad joked. "He's got the whole street thinking he's malnourished." I lugged Everest up into a cuddle which he put up with for as long as he could bear before twisting out of my arms and lolloping towards the kitchen, hopeful of a midnight feast. It had felt so nice to have everyone at home again. Everyone happy. I had forgotten what it used to be like, and I felt this twist in my tummy as I remembered.

Just before Dad had moved out it hadn't been like this, I reminded myself. It wasn't happy and relaxed or natural. But remembering that my family had once been so happy made me feel sad. Perhaps it was because I was tired and stressed by what had happened at Nydia's house, perhaps it was the excitement and drama of being arrested, but as I watched Mum and Dad talking in the kitchen just as they used to when I was little, I found myself wishing that all three of us were still properly together and that those difficult angry years had not happened at all.

But it might as well have been a wish made on some birthday candles because along with the swimming pool and motorbike I'd hoped for from the age of seven, it was another wish that would never come true.

We'd only been in a little while when I said I wanted to go to bed. I wasn't tired, but as I went up Mum was making Dad another cup of tea and I wanted to give them time alone to see if they felt the same way I did when they remembered what it used to be like to be in our family.

Plus I wanted to eavesdrop on what they were talking about.

So I went up the stairs as loudly and as heavily as I could and then crept down as quietly and as lightly as possible, skipping over the stair with a creak and settling on the second from bottom step. As I listened, the draft from under the front door crept around my ankles making my toes numb with cold.

"I don't know what to think, Frank," Mum had said

wearily. "This sort of behaviour – running off like that – it's not like our Ruby."

"Yes," Dad had said, "but this sort of life, mixing with film stars and going to premieres isn't like our Ruby either. Maybe we are pushing her too far; maybe she's not ready for this kind of pressure yet. You hear about it all the time – about child stars going off the rails. And I don't like the look of that Sean either; he looks like trouble to me."

"Actually," Mum said, "I don't think it's Sean that's the problem as much as his father. The gossip is that the man only looks at his son as a cash machine. I don't think he cares how the boy feels as long as he can make money out of him. Do you know the poor boy hasn't had a holiday in two years!" I thought of Sean, his head bowed, standing in the corridor just before we left the party. It was funny how almost every girl in the world could know so much about him, including the name of his first pet (Bunny) and his favourite colour (green) and not know how unhappy he was, how much he hated living the life so many children dream about having.

"We haven't pushed her like that, Frank," Mum said. "We supported her with what she wants to do, encouraged and helped her, but we've never forced her."

Dad said nothing for a moment or two, but I could hear the sound of a teaspoon chiming against the rim of a mug.

"Perhaps," Dad said cautiously, "what she wants isn't good for her. Perhaps we should think about stopping her from acting until she's old enough to handle it properly."

I had to clamp my hand over my mouth to keep myself from crying out. You accidentally steal a few diamonds while secretly leaving a party and suddenly everybody thinks you've gone to pieces. *Personally, I thought to myself, considering my boyfriend's dumped me over nothing and my best friend hates me for, well, being me, I was surprisingly together and well behaved.*

"Do you think," Mum said, without ruling the forcing-me-to-stop-acting option immediately out, "that it's everything that's happened in the last few months? To us as a family, I mean. Maybe that's what all this 'acting out' is about. Maybe she is attention-seeking."

I dropped my head into my hands and shut my eyes in despair. OK, so I'd left a party without telling anyone where I was going and had gone round to Nydia's, but factor out the diamonds and the film star I took with me and then really it wasn't *especially* bad behaviour. Why couldn't anybody else see that?

Maybe Mum and Dad splitting up was still there at the bottom of everything I felt and did, because although I tried not to think about it too much, and I tried to do my best to be fine with it, perhaps I didn't realise exactly how it had changed me and everything around me. It was only then, in those last few minutes of that strange and difficult day, that I had allowed myself to think and feel anything about what had happened to their marriage at all. Most of the time I kept the reality of their impending divorce locked up inside me. But sometimes, like now, the hurt and the pain would seep out and I knew that things would never be the same.

My parents would never be the same parents I grew up with, the wise, invincible people who were always right and who always made everything all right. As much as I loved them I just didn't believe in them in the same way any more, and if I was really honest I didn't completely trust them the way I used to before they pulled my world to pieces around me. And because of that, I would never completely be the same daughter; I couldn't be. Because now I knew that sometimes, even if it was the last thing they wanted to do, they would inevitably let me down.

But still, that wasn't why I had left the party and got into trouble, not really, and it would be wrong to blame it on my parents getting divorced. And it had nothing to do with the pressure of shooting a movie, which even though it had its stressful moments was still the best and most brilliant thing I could ever do.

I had done that because I had been seriously stupid. Even more stupid than usual. And I had not thought through the consequences of my actions at all. I considered running into the kitchen and clearing it up straight away, but before I could Dad was speaking again.

"I don't know, Janice," I heard him say, his voice slow and tired.

"What should we do?" Mum asked him.

"When things have settled down a bit," Dad said, "we'll have a talk with her. Find out what she's really thinking. Talk about her future."

"Both of us together, you mean?" My mum said.

"Yes," Dad said. "Both of us, of course. I'm still her father." Then I heard Dad's chair scrape back and I bolted up the stairs and crouched around the corner on the landing as I watched him go. After Mum had shut the front door on him she stood with her back to it, her head hanging for a moment.

"I don't know," she said to Everest, who was asleep, perched seriously precariously on the telephone shelf over the radiator. "I just don't know."

Join the club, I thought to myself as I huddled under my duvet that night. I thought about when I was a little girl and how everything had seemed so simple and easy. That night I had this dream – it was as if I was walking through a maze, and every day, with every step I took, I got older and the maze got more difficult and more complicated. I kept on taking wrong turnings and running into dead ends. The further I went the more difficult it became to go the right way. That's what my dream felt like.

Except that when I woke up I still couldn't see how I was ever going to find my way out again.

Sitting at the breakfast table with Mum, I folded the paper shut so that I didn't have to look at the photo of me and Sean kissing. Captured like that it made it look as if it was the kind of kiss that went on for ever, not a peck that was over in a second. And where Sean had fleetingly put his hand on my waist – well, let's just say from the angle that this photo was taken it looks like I've got a very, *very* high waist. And worse still, next to the article about me there was a column by some old decrepit agony aunt about the dangers of underage sex!

Right next to mine and Sean's photo. It was mortifying.

A photo of a second-long kiss had somehow morphed into a scandal about illegal marriages and sparked a national debate on teenage sex, and I knew nothing about teenage sex; I had just got the hang of teenage kissing, and that was quite enough for me for at least another ten years. But now the whole country would think differently. And worst of all, Danny would be looking at that photo too this morning, and reading that article. And when he did he'd be even more cross and stupid and annoying and further away from being my Danny than ever. I didn't know if the thought made me upset or annoyed.

Danny *should* know me well enough to trust me. He should realise that everything in that paper, including the photo, was some kind of half-truth or implied lie. And he should try to remember that we were Danny and Ruby of London, not Romeo and Juliet of Verona. If we all calmed down a bit and thought things through then it didn't have to turn out to be a tragedy.

"It's not fair," I told Mum, sounding like next-door's toddler and feeling a bit like him too. Mum raised her eyebrows at me and pressed her mouth into a very thin line. I wondered if I should tell her I'd heard her talking to Dad last night and that she didn't have to worry, I wasn't going off the rails like a child star, I was just having a very small wobble like a thirteen-year-old girl. But one more look at her face convinced me that adding eavesdropping to my list of misdemeanours was not a good plan.

"I'm sorry, Mum," I said, nodding at the tightly-closed paper. "I didn't mean for any of it to happen; it just did. I acted like an idiot."

Mum rubbed her forehead with her fingers and then pushed them through her newly red hair. She still had gold nail varnish on. It looked funny with her usual Mum clothes.

"I'm not thrilled about seeing my daughter in the tabloid press kissing a boy," she said evenly. "But I do know that there's nothing in that story. Or any of that other rubbish. I was there, Ruby, I saw the so-called kiss, and besides, I know how Sean is with you, he treats you like a kid sister. Maybe he should have thought about what he was doing, going along with your silly plan to just leave the premiere, especially as he is older than you." Mum pursed her lips. "I would have words with him, only I'm sure the poor boy will get more than enough from his father."

I thought about the last time I had seen Sean last night. As I had been caught up in the middle of a family hug, I had just a glimpse of Sean out of the corner of my eye getting dragged by his father towards the lift. The look on his dad's face was one that I had never seen on my own father's: it was one of pure cold fury, and it made me feel sick inside. When I saw that look on his face I felt afraid for Sean, and I prayed that whatever his punishment would be, it could not be as bad as I imagined. It seemed so wrong that a newspaper could print all that rubbish about me, make up all those stories about Sean, when none of them, nobody in the world hardly, knew what his real life was like.

"This," Mum patted the paper firmly, "comes with fame, Ruby, and if you are to continue along this path you'll have to learn to live with it. And at your age do your level best to stay out of the papers. Take a leaf out of Imogene's book – she never compromises herself. Never."

"I will. I promise," I said solemnly.

"It's not even the diamonds that are that much of a problem," Mum said, a tiny smile breaking up her frown lines. "Everybody knows you didn't mean to go off in them. Even De Beers thought it was quite funny in the end. Once they had stopped panicking and demanding a swat team. I spoke to Lisa and she says they are actually quite pleased with the publicity." I gave a little shrug.

"I really forgot I was wearing them," I said. Mum's face fell again.

"What worries me, Ruby," she said, "what upset me more than anything, was that you left, ran away from me without telling me where you were going or who with. I thought I could trust you. If I hadn't I would have never left your side. It would have been so easy to just tell me that you wanted to go to Nydia's. I would have taken you! Instead for quite a while there I was so terrified. Terrified that you'd been kidnapped, taken by someone who wanted the diamonds or... or..." Mum's face clouded over and she bit her lips hard, "someone who might want to hurt you, Ruby."

"But I wasn't," I said, smiling like an idiot and waggling jazz hands at her. "Look, I'm fine!"

"I didn't know that," Mum said. "You didn't tell me. I was worried sick, Ruby."

I tried to think of an excuse or reason for what I had done, but nothing came. Since I had started working on *The Lost Treasure of King Arthur*, the days had flown by so quickly that they had all jumbled up, and sometimes I felt like I couldn't tell what was real and what wasn't – on and off the set. I was already almost halfway through the shoot, but it still felt like it had only just begun; just as I was getting used to it, it was already finishing. I thought it was enough to make anyone a little bit erratic.

I pushed my chair back and went and stood behind Mum. I leaned over her and put my arms around her neck, resting my chin on her shoulder.

"I was just being stupid, Mum," I said after a while. "I'm not an expert in child psychology, but I promise you I'm not going off the rails and it's not because of you and Dad. You don't have to force me to stop acting or anything like that!" Mum gave me a sharp look over her shoulder but didn't say anything. "It was just me being stupid. And I won't ever do that to you again, I promise you."

Mum put her arms up and gave me a sort of upside-down hug.

"I can't do anything right," I said, going back to my chair and sitting down. "Nydia's fallen out with me because she's angry with me for getting the part in the film."

"That doesn't sound like Nydia," Mum said, sipping her tea. "She's usually so supportive. Especially when she's just got that TV part; she doesn't have to be jealous of you." I picked up a pot of jam and tried to open the lid. It was stuck fast. I knew how it felt.

"I know," I said. "But she's not like Nydia; she's

completely different. It's like I'm not even talking to her but to her angry twin instead."

"You'll work things out with Nydia," Mum said confidently. "You two have been friends for too long not to."

I sighed; I wish I felt as confident as she did. Nydia and I seemed to have gone from being almost exactly the same as each other to totally and completely different people almost overnight.

"Maybe," I said, unconvinced. "But even if we did, Danny still wouldn't want to be my boyfriend any more."

"What?" Mum exclaimed. "*Why?*"

"He thinks I fancy Sean," I said. "And after he's read that stuff in the paper, well then…"

"You did tell him that you don't fancy Sean, didn't you?" Mum asked me.

"I did," I said, picking up the paper and opening it at the photo again, "but he didn't believe me and now he's never going to, is he?"

Mum took the paper from me, folded it, took it to the paper recycling bin under the sink and dropped it in.

"If he's more likely to believe in that than you," Mum said, nodding at the bin, "then he's not worth worrying about, Ruby. Don't give the silly boy a second thought."

"I know," I said miserably. But there was a problem

about not worrying over Danny or giving him a second thought, despite his foolish jealous behaviour. Quite a big problem.

I was still in love with him, of course.

"Action!"

Chapter Eighteen

Imogene Grant, double Oscar-winning actress, was making me a cheese and salad sandwich in her Winnebago. She'd caught up with me as I had been going back to my trailer and lightly dropping an arm around my shoulders asked me if I wanted to have lunch with her. I asked Mum, who said it was fine as she had a lot to do anyway. I didn't know what lot of things she could have to do on a film set when her main job was looking after me, but I didn't ask her. She seemed in a good mood again and I didn't want to spoil that.

And as I watched Imogene wash and chop some salad I wondered how on earth I, Ruby Parker, had got to be here. And I wondered how different my life would have been if I had never been chosen at the age of six to play the part of Angel MacFarley in *Kensington Heights*.

I would never have known Nydia I supposed, or Danny – but seeing as neither one of them was talking to me any more I wondered if that mattered. Then again,

I told myself, I would never have made friends with Sean, acted with Jeremy Fort or had Imogene Grant make me a cheese and salad sandwich, and all before the age of fourteen.

Imogene put the sandwich on a plate and set it down on the table before me. She slid opposite me with her own sandwich and looked at me.

"So," she said. "How are you doing?"

I looked into her world-famous velvet-brown eyes.

"I was just thinking, what if none of this had happened to me?" I said, gesturing around me at the interior of the Winnebago but really meaning my whole, strange life. "I was wondering if I would have a different life, a normal life, parents who were still married, a best friend who still liked me, a boyfriend who didn't get jealous over nothing. I was wondering if I would be normal."

Imogene smiled and took a sip of her water.

"Ruby," she said, "the life that you just described isn't normal. Real friends always fall out one time or another. Adult relationships have difficult times, sometimes so difficult that they can't be mended. And sometimes when you really love someone it's very hard not to be jealous, even if you know it's wrong. *That's* normal life, the kind of life that happens to a lot of girls your age all around the world. The only difference is that most of those girls will never get arrested by armed police and find their photo in the national press the next day!" Imogene smiled and watched me as she took a dainty bite of her sandwich. Vaguely, I wondered if there was a school somewhere that taught movie stars how to eat without getting mayonnaise down their tops.

"You know what?" she told me. "You should feel lucky." I gave a dry bark of a laugh, but Imogene persisted. "You should! A lot of kids in show business don't have what you have. They don't have a normal school where they can make friends good enough to fall out with, or have the chance to get to know a boy long enough to date him. And as for parents – well, look at Sean. He never sees his mom, which let me tell you breaks her heart. And as for his father, well, he's just a..." Imogene seemed to stop herself from using the word she wanted to. "He's a very *difficult* man."

I nodded, that was true and, I thought miserably, even *more* true than Imogene knew. Everybody knew that Pat Rivers was a difficult man to deal with, but did they know exactly how miserable he made his own son in private?

That morning Sean had not been his usual happy-go-lucky self at all. Oh, he had switched on his starriness for his scenes, but it had blinked out again the moment the cameras stopped rolling and he saw his father at the edge of the set waiting for him, tapping his crocodile-skin shoes impatiently. And I noticed that some of the dark and vivid bruises on Sean's arms and legs were not applied by the make-up department.

"How did you get those?" I asked Sean as soon as I got a chance.

He shrugged but didn't look me in the eye.

"I don't know," he said. "Messing around I guess. I went out on my skateboard yesterday." I was fairly certain he was lying.

As I watched Sean go without saying goodbye, his head down and his shoulders slumped, I thought of how Sean had been in the corridor just before we left the premiere party, and I had a horrible feeling that maybe this Sean, this down, hurt and sad Sean *was* his usual self. And that maybe the happy, adventurous, spontaneous Sean I thought I had got to know was just another act, a brave front.

"Poor Sean," I said, more to myself than to Imogene.

"And look at *me*," Imogene continued.

"What about you?" I asked her. "You're perfect."

Imogene grinned and shook her head.

"Nobody is perfect," she said. "Least of all me."

"Yes, you are!" I protested. "I bet you were born perfect. I bet you were never lumpy or spotty or greasy, were you?" I shrugged and smiled at her. "It doesn't matter; I'm not holding it against you or anything. It's just that some people in the world are perfectly perfect and some, like me, are not and never will be. I'm learning to accept it." I sighed; that wasn't exactly true. I was still hoping for a late surge that might get me from average-if-not-ugly ducking to drop-dead-gorgeous swan before I turned eighteen, but I had to face it, time was running out.

Imogene nipped at her lips as she thought for a moment about what I'd said and then she said, "Wait there a minute, I want to show you something."

She slid out from her seat opposite and went into her bedroom. She returned a few moments later with a photo album and sat down again, but this time next to me.

She rested the red leather album on the table top and patted it fondly.

"I take this with me wherever I go," she told me as she opened the thick pages. "To remind me of who I am. Look, I want to show you a photo."

She thumbed through the stiff pages until she found the one she was looking for. It was an image of her from her first breakthrough role as a Vegas street kid in a thriller called *Boiling Point*. She only had a small part but every critic said she acted the other well-known stars off the screen.

I looked carefully at the photo of Imogene; she was just a bit older than me when it was taken. Shot against the hot red of a setting desert sun she looked incredible, almost alight, so fragile and delicate that you thought you might be able to see through her. But I still didn't know why she was showing me the photo.

"Were you forced into acting too?" I asked her, frowning. Imogene shook her head.

"No." She studied the photo for a second longer and ran her thumb down the edge of her slight thirteen-year-old figure. "I didn't know it then, but when this photo was taken I was actually dying."

"*Dying!*" I stared at her and then the photo in horror. "What of?"

Imogene thought for a moment and then uncovered the left-hand page of the album that her forearm had been resting on. "Here, let me show you another photo," she said.

This time the photo was of an awkward and unhappy-looking girl posing in a very frilly and far too tight pink dress. She looked as if the smile she was giving the camera had been hammered on with nails. It took me a few seconds to realise that the girl was Imogene too.

"But you're..." I stopped myself from finishing the sentence by biting my lip.

"Fat?" Imogene finished for me.

I nodded.

"No one forced me into acting, or into film," Imogene told me. "I wanted it; it was *all* that I wanted. And being in school shows or the local drama group wasn't enough for me. I wanted all of *this*..." This time she gestured around her at the Winnebago and I knew she meant her movie-star life. "And the cold truth of the matter in this shallow business, Ruby, is that fat kids, no matter how talented they are, hardly ever get it." Imogene smiled with a kind of fond sadness at the pink-dress photo. "So without telling anyone I put myself on a diet. First of all I just watched what I ate, cut out candy and cakes, but when that didn't work fast enough I ate less and less unil I actually couldn't bear the sight of food. The thought of it in my mouth made me want to be sick. I made excuses not to eat with my family, and if I couldn't get out of it I'd leave whatever my mom gave me, saying I'd eaten earlier, or that I just wasn't hungry. If I did have to eat in front of them, I forced down a few mouthfuls and as soon as I could I'd make myself sick.

"Ew," I said, wrinkling up my nose. I looked at beautiful, graceful Ms Grant. I just couldn't imagine her doing anything so... ugly.

"It was gross," Imogene said. "It made my breath stink and my teeth started to rot, but I didn't think about that. All I thought about was being thin." She tapped her prefect white teeth. "These are ceramic overlays. Anyway, I got thinner and thinner until I looked exactly like this." She tapped the *Boiling Point* photo with her fingernail. "And I knew I was right to be doing what I was doing because I started getting jobs. And the people who counted started noticing me, so I kept going because I thought the thinner I was the more they would want me, and it seemed to be true." Imogene shook her head.

"But whatever talent or ability Hollywood saw in me they still didn't see the one thing that I saw." She pointed at the pink-dress girl again. "Even when I was at my thinnest, whenever I looked in the mirror I'd see her, that dumb fat girl looking back at me. I wasn't ever happy. I was never thin enough."

There was a moment's silence as Imogene and I stared from photo to photo and I thought about Nydia and her secret diet. I felt a sharp twist of fear knot in my tummy as I worried that she could go too far just like Imogene had.

"But you didn't die," I said in a small voice. "Dieting can't really make you die, can it?"

Imogene shrugged. "It can; if you let it take over you like I did it can become a serious disease," she said. "I was shooting my next film after *Boiling Point*. It was a much bigger, more important part so I was literally eating nothing at all so I could look good in front of the camera." Imogene sighed wistfully.

"I'd only been on set a couple of days when I collapsed. I got rushed into hospital. They put all sorts of tubes into me. I had to have my heart monitored in case it failed. I got fed through a tube in my nose." I wrinkled up my nose and rubbed it at the thought of having a tube inserted in it. "After a few days when I was stable again the doctor told me if I carried on as I was I'd be dead within a year. That scared me," Imogene said with a little smile.

"That would scare me too," I said.

"But if I'm really honest, I think what scared me even more was that I got dropped from the film. I was told I couldn't work again until I was healthy and under control. That was what really woke me up: I was more afraid of giving up my dream than I was of dying. I think that was what made me accept the treatment and the counselling. And when it was out in the open, when my parents knew at last, it felt as if a sort of tent had been lifted from above me, and I could breathe and feel the sun on my face again. It took me a long time to get it under control, years to teach myself to eat properly again. I didn't make another movie until I was nineteen." Imogene seemed to look inwards for a moment as if she were watching those memories play inside her head.

"*New York Angel*," I said, remembering the title of her second film. "Your first Oscar."

Imogene nodded and shut the album, resting both of her forearms on it as if she were afraid something – the past maybe – might try and escape.

"Why did you tell me all this?" I asked her. She shrugged.

"Because I trust you and because you remind me a lot of myself when I was your age..."

"Do I?" I said, and must have sounded a bit worried because Imogene put her arm around me and hugged me. "Don't worry," she said. "I don't mean I think you're going to do something crazy like I did. It's just that now is an important time for you, Ruby. You have a lot of talent – everybody thinks so. If this film does well things could go crazy for you – you could suddenly find yourself being pulled in all sorts of directions. If that happens I want you to think very carefully about what you are doing. Pause and take a breath. Don't worry about being perfect. No one in this business is perfect. All we are is very good at hiding our imperfections, and sometimes we get so obsessed with it we start to destroy ourselves. It's a real danger, Ruby. The best thing you can do is to just be you, otherwise this industry will burn you out before you've even begun."

"Like Sean," I said quietly.

"It would seem so," Imogene said with a tiny smile. "It's easy to let this life get on top of you when you are your age, especially if you haven't got the right guidance. And it's easy to let things get out of perspective and lose sight of who you are. Just remember the best thing you have going for you right now is your school, your friends, and most of all your parents. Keep those steady and they will keep you steady. And never forget how lucky you are."

I thought for a moment.

"I am lucky," I said, sounding quite surprised. "I had forgotten how lucky I am."

"I thought so," Imogene said.

I thought about Nydia and Danny, Mum and Dad, and even Sean, and all the things I thought were so terrible in my life. When I thought about it none of them were things I couldn't make better somehow. It was just knowing where and how to start.

Suddenly I remembered something that Imogene had said earlier.

"You said that Sean's mum's heart was broken because of not seeing him," I said. Imogene nodded and raised a questioning eyebrow. "Do you know her?"

"I used to," Imogene said. "We worked together once a long time ago. This is the first time I've worked with Sean. It's horrible that the rumours about his father could be true."

"Well, if you can trust me, I can trust you," I said, hoping I wasn't betraying Sean by what I was about to tell her. "There's something that Sean's mum really needs to know."

"Action!"

Chapter Nineteen

As I walked over to Sean's trailer, wanting to tell him what I had told Imogene, I was stopped in my tracks by an unexpected but familiar voice.

"Ruby! It's me!" I turned around and stared at Anne-Marie.

"Hello?" I said, not quite believing my eyes.

"It's me, I've come to visit you," she said excitedly. "Daddy is back home for a week and he's got some business here so I pestered him until he said I could come too. Brilliant thing emotional blackmail, but I suppose there have to be some perks to having permanently absent parents."

"What about school?" I asked her.

"Daddy said I could take the afternoon off," she said. "It's only games and geography and they don't really count, Daddy says."

Anne-Marie hooked her arm through mine.

"I thought," she told me, dropping her head on to my

shoulder for a moment, "that after everything you've been through you could use a friend to talk to. What with Nydia not speaking to you – or to anyone very much for that matter – and Danny chucking you, I thought you must feel terrible." Anne-Marie gave my arm a little squeeze.

"Honestly," she said, "I can't believe the way he's acting. I mean, I thought he'd be miserable for weeks and weeks, at least! But going straight out on a date with Jade Caruso – what on earth is he thinking? It's *obvious* that Sean isn't interested in *you*." Anne-Marie glanced hopefully around the empty lot. "Is he around by the way?"

I stopped dead in my tracks and tried hard to remember what Imogene had told me – that I was lucky, lucky, lucky.

"He went on a date with Jade?" I asked Anne-Marie.

She clapped her hand over her mouth, her blue eyes wide with horror.

"Oh, no," she moaned. "I'm so stupid. You must think I'm a cow! I just thought you'd know already, I don't know why. Nydia would usually have told you but she's not talking to you, is she? I didn't mean to tell you like that. I was just excited about being here and I don't know what I was thinking."

I shook my head. "It doesn't matter," I said, keeping my voice steady. "At least I know where I stand now."

"Oh, babe," Anne Marie said and she clasped me in a tight hug.

"Let's go somewhere," she said in my ear as she hugged me. "Just the two of us and have really good girly... Oh, hi, Sean!" Anne-Marie let go of me suddenly as if I were a hot brick, and fluttered her lashes at Sean.

I turned around and gave Sean a half-hearted smile, completely forgetting what it was I was supposed to tell him.

"Annie!" he called out to Anne-Marie, using a nickname which everyone else in the world was forbidden from calling her. "My dance partner's here – excellent!"

"She's come to visit me," I said rather obviously, still reeling from the news that Danny was dating Jade. "Only I've got to be on set in ten minutes, Anne-Marie. I can't talk now – I'll be at least two or three hours. Maybe you'd better find your dad and get him to take you home."

"Or," Sean said, carefully casual, "I've got nothing on till a night shoot on location later on, unless you count classes with Fran Francisco, which I don't. Dad's in town doing yet another new deal, so if you like I could give you a tour while you wait for Ruby?"

"Oh," Anne-Marie said coolly, giving me a wink. "I suppose that would be OK."

I watched the pair walk off together, feeling a bit miserable and left out.

"I'll see you in my trailer later then?" I called out. "Mum will be there so just knock. Sean will show you where it is."

"OK, Ruby," she called back. "And just remember, the show must…"

"Go on," I finished for her under my breath. I turned on my heel and made my way towards the set. At least for the next few hours I wouldn't have to remember how lucky I was.

I'd be too busy fighting my evil father to the death, suspended above a vat of boiling molten lava.

It was dark by the time I got out of wardrobe and I didn't expect Anne-Marie to still be waiting, but she was. I could hear her laughter before I even got to my little Winnebago.

She and Sean were sitting at the little table playing

cards. Anne-Marie's cheeks were flushed and her eyes shone brightly. They looked as if they had been laughing since the moment I left them, and I couldn't help feeling an ungracious pang of jealousy.

I flopped down next to Anne-Marie, exhausted, and actually quite wishing that neither of them was there.

"Where's Mum?" I asked through a yawn.

"She said she'd be back in ten minutes to take you to the flat," Anne-Marie said, not quite answering my question. "Daddy will be here in a minute too."

I glanced at them.

"You two look like you've had fun," I said, my voice a heavy flat monotone.

Sean gave me a sympathetic smile.

"I'm afraid we did," he said. He sighed deeply and looked at his watch. "But now I've got to go. It was good to see you again, Annie," he said. "I hope I see you again before I go."

"I hope so too," Anne-Marie said, letting her cool façade slip, and sounding rather wistful for a moment.

"Well, whatever," I said, feeling a bit grumpy. "Hope it goes all right tonight, Sean." Sean shrugged.

"It usually does," he said as he left. "Acting is the one thing I can't seem to get wrong." There was a rush of cold air as he opened and closed the trailer door.

After he had gone I could see Anne-Marie trying her best to turn down her excitement as far as she could until she was able to rearrange her features in an expression which more matched my own. She patted my forearm quite firmly, so that it stung a little bit.

"How are you doing?" she asked me with a little pout, which made me smile for some reason. When it came to girl talk, even after months of being friends, Anne-Marie still wasn't a patch on Nydia. But she was here, even if it was partly to see Sean, and she was really trying. I appreciated that.

"I'm fine," I said heavily. "I mean, I am sad because I really liked Danny and, well... I just don't know how this all happened. Over nothing at all really."

"I don't think that article in the paper helped," Anne-Marie said seriously, before giggling a little bit. "Or that photo."

I screwed up my face as I remembered it.

"I know," I said. "But Jade Caruso? She is really pretty, I suppose – in an obvious way."

"Pretty evil," Anne-Marie said, and I managed to laugh. "Anyway, he doesn't really like her. He's just acting like an idiot again. Like the old Danny before you got to know him and brought him over from the dark side – grumpy and sullen and always hanging around on his own. He hasn't really talked to Jade since the date or on it, if what Michael Henderson says is true. Whereas she hasn't stopped talking about *him*." Anne-Marie rolled her eyes and sighed. "The trouble with Danny is that he *likes* things to be complicated. He should be more like Sean; Sean likes the simple things in life."

"What, like you?" I asked. Anne-Marie pursed her lips for a moment before extending them into a smile.

"I'm letting you get away with that because you're depressed," she said.

"Hang on," I said. Suddenly I saw exactly how to fix things with Danny.

"What?" Anne-Marie asked.

"Well, it's obvious really – you know Sean doesn't fancy me because he fancies you! All you have to do is tell Danny and then everything will be fine. He can be all humble and apologise to me, I can be all gracious and forgive him and we can get back to normal again." Anne-Marie's smile froze on her lips.

"Except that Sean doesn't fancy me," she said, tossing her blonde curls back over her shoulder as she said it.

"He does!" I said. "It's obvious!"

Anne Marie shook her head.

"He doesn't fancy me and I don't fancy him either,

actually." I looked hard at Anne-Marie. It was obvious that she was lying, but I knew what had happened: she had told Sean she liked him and he had ever so politely and sweetly told her he wasn't interested. He probably told her that he couldn't have a girlfriend; he was never in one place long enough. And even though he must have let her down ever so gently judging by how well they were getting on when I came back, Anne-Marie didn't want me to know. I suppose I couldn't blame her.

"Oh," I said. "OK."

"And anyway, you shouldn't have to prove to Danny that Sean is with someone else so that he'll believe you," Anne-Marie said, getting quite fiery. "He should just believe you! But then again I suppose boys do sometimes need things spelling out for them, don't they?" She nodded decisively. "Danny needs a good talking to and I'm going to give it to him and make him see that he's wrong."

"Danny isn't good at being wrong," I said hesitantly.

"Yeah, well," Anne-Marie said, lifting her chin a little, "I'm worse."

"And what about Nydia?" I said. "I'm worried about her."

"Why?" Anne-Marie asked me crossly, not knowing, I supposed, about why Nydia was acting so strangely.

"She's got nothing to be so miserable about. She's got a part on TV – that's more than most of us. She's just totally overreacting to you getting this part, and if anybody should be jealous and bitter it's me, not her! I'm really surprised by how she's being with me as well as you. I'm a bit cross actually." Anne-Marie drummed her forefinger on the table top to make her point.

"Still," I said carefully, "will you talk to her gently to see how she is – just in case it's something else that's upsetting her? She won't answer my calls."

"OK, I will, I *suppose*," Anne-Marie said, with a theatrical sigh. "I do quite miss the old Nydia. School is a bit boring with both of you missing. I've got no one to torment, and at least when I'm hanging around with you two it makes me look really good."

"Thank you, Annie," I said.

And I gave her a hug before she could punch me.

Chapter Twenty

In the end I saw Danny before I saw Anne-Marie.

It all came as a bit of a surprise, and it happened so quickly that I hardly had time to catch my breath, and I certainly would never have guessed that things would turn out the way that they did.

The morning after my visit with Anne-Marie, Lisa interrupted Sean and me during a tuition period with Fran Francisco, who wasn't nearly as pleased about the distraction as we were.

"Who is Sindy Torrington, Ruby?" Lisa asked me over the top of her clipboard. I frowned at her.

"Sindy Torrington," I said with a shrug, "is or rather was Shona Mackay, a character from Aussie soap *Bush Patrol*, that is until her character got eaten by a crocodile and she left the show to pursue a pop career. Why?" Lisa grinned at Sean and me.

"She's broken her leg," she said. "Isn't that great?"

I looked at Sean, who looked as confused as I did.

"Well, I mean, I was never a fan but…" I said uncertainly.

"She was due to present an award at the National Soap Awards, which is being broadcast live to the nation tonight!" Lisa told us excitedly, jiggling so that her beads click-clacked. Sean and I exchanged a mystified look.

I wasn't confused about the awards; I knew perfectly well that they were going to be on tonight, because after all I had received an invitation which I had declined due to work commitments. What I didn't get was why Lisa was so happy about one of the presenters suffering an injury that would surely ruin her dance routines.

"And that's good *why*?" Sean asked Lisa, clearly as mystified as me.

"Because," Lisa said, "it means they need a replacement, or should I say replacements, for her urgently and – they want you two!" Lisa gave us a mini round of applause, and Fran Francisco checked her watch. "Both of you have been asked, *begged*, to step in to replace this Sindy woman and give the award she was going to present. You two are all the rage since your little escapade in the papers. And it will be great pre-publicity for the film; there's nothing like an on-set romance to get the press interested."

"And this is *nothing* like an on-set romance," Sean said a little crossly.

"I know that and you guys know that," Lisa said. "But *they* don't have to know that."

"Actually," I began, "I'd prefer it..." but Lisa was already in full flow, talking over me. And if there was one thing I had learned recently it was not to interrupt her when she was in full flow. It was a bit like waking up a sleepwalker in the middle of a dream – who knew what damage it could do?

"Now, Sean, your dad's OK'd it in principle, but he's negotiating on the appearance fee and, Ruby, your mum and your agent are very happy with the terms, so all you have to do is say yes. It will be so sweet..."

"Bleugh," Sean said, sticking his tongue out and crossing his eyes at me.

" ... and perfect!" Lisa said, ignoring him. "Because you two are emerging talent..."

"Hey," Sean said, raising his hand. I was sure that he knew just as I did that Lisa did not like to be interrupted, but unlike me he was not afraid of annoying her. Sean was not afraid of anything – except his father. "I am not sweet, and I *have* emerged, thank you very much."

"Well, maybe," Lisa said. "But anyway, it's appropriate because the award you'll be presenting is for the Best Newcomer in a British Soap."

"Oh?" I said, getting a funny feeling in my tummy.

The sort of feeling you sometimes get when you know exactly what the person you are talking to is about to say next, even if you don't want to hear it.

"Who's nominated?" I asked her. In theory, if Danny had been nominated I would have known about it, but if I remembered correctly, nominations for these awards were only announced a week before the actual ceremony. And I had barely spoken to Danny except to argue with him. And it would be typical of him to keep something like this to himself. I held my breath and crossed my fingers.

"Let me see," Lisa scanned her clipboard. "There's Alison Higgins, never heard of her, Jamie Jameson, never heard of him, Tatiana Khan – oh, now, she's quite good actually – and Danny Harvey. Hey, he's from *Kensington Heights*, your old show! Moody good-looking kid – do you know him?"

I looked at Sean, who gave me a conciliatory pat on the back.

"You could say that," I said, happy for Danny and upset for me all at once.

"Cool, let's hope he wins, hey?" Lisa said, checking her clipboard again. "Now you have to be at the BBC Theatre by six for transmission at eight. You both have scenes this afternoon so we'll get you dressed and made up here before you go, OK? Our good friend Tallulah is sourcing you something to wear. Are you all set?"

"Yes," Sean and I chorused unenthusiastically.

"Great, now get back to your school work; your life depends on knowing how to do fractions. Oh, and one other thing, Ruby."

"What's that?" I asked Lisa.

"This time, you'll be wearing *fake* diamonds, OK?"

It's been an amazing few months for rising star Danny Harvey. Since appearing as a guest character in *Kensington Heights* he has been given a long-term contract by the producers and has seen his storylines and character profile grow and grow.

And Danny's brooding but vulnerable character is fast becoming a firm favourite with *Kensington Heights'* younger viewers – his poster replacing his co-star Justin de Souza's in thousand of bedrooms across the country.

And now, as the end of the year approaches, Danny has been nominated for the Best Newcomer at the British Soap Awards. There's stiff competition in his category, but as far as the team at *HIYA! BYE-A!* is concerned, Dan is the Man for this award!

Chapter Twenty-one

"Action!"

Mum, Pat Rivers, Sean and I
sat in the back of the limo as we waited for the security
check at the BBC Theatre.

All the way we had sat in awkward, difficult silence.
My mum had tried to talk to Sean's dad a couple of
times. She asked him how he liked Britain and did he
miss California. At one point she said he must be so
proud of his son, which was the only time I heard any
sound at all from Sean, a sort of strangulated, muffled
laugh. But although Pat Rivers answered Mum most
politely and always called her "ma'am", it was clear that
he didn't really want to waste his breath on her because,
after all, there was nothing that my mum could do for
him.

That was pretty bad, but not quite as bad as the
dress Tallulah Banks had tried to make me wear earlier
that evening. I knew she had been waiting for the
moment she could get revenge on me for ripping

Imogene's gold gown, and finally her moment had come.

"Don't want you in anything too adult, hey, Ruby," she'd said as she produced the most hideous dress I have ever seen in my life and presented it to me. It was like all of your worst bridesmaid's dress nightmares rolled into one and it looked as if Tallulah had picked it based solely on how terrible it would make me look.

Firstly, it was lemon yellow, and the minute I put it on I looked like a lemon too, because the colour reflected on to my skin and made me look jaundiced. Secondly, it had a *sash*: the sort of sash you dream of when you are about four, but one you'd cheerfully hang yourself with rather than be seen in public actually wearing at the age of thirteen. *It tied in a bow at the side!*

Thirdly, it had a full, frilly skirt. And fourthly, it had puff sleeves.

It was yellow-dress hell.

"Perfect," Tallulah said with a cruel smile, as I gingerly came out of the dressing room. "Just the effect I wanted."

I stared at myself miserably in the mirror, imagining the soap awards' eight million viewers at home and audience of celebrities – which included my ex-boyfriend, thank you very much – laughing themselves sick when I came on stage looking like a lemon meringue.

I wondered if I was brave enough to complain and make a fuss. But I think I used up all of my limited rebellious resources when I ran off with the diamonds, because one look at Tallulah's face told me I was not nearly brave enough.

Feeling like an exploded banana soufflé I trudged next door to where Sean had just finished getting dressed.

He was in a white suit with an ice-blue T-shirt underneath, and *he* looked utterly cool and handsome.

"No one told me it was fancy dress!" he said when he saw me. He was trying to be his usual charming self, but this dress knocked even him off balance.

"I know," I said unhappily. "It's gruesome."

"Then why did you put it on?" he asked me in disbelief.

"Because I haven't got a choice!" I told him. "My only consolation is that I'll only be on national TV for about fifteen seconds and will mostly be standing behind a podium."

Sean looked sceptical.

"No," he said.

"No what?" I said.

"No, you are not wearing that!" He took my hand and began walking. "If I *have* to be having a fake romance with you then you at least have to look halfway decent. Follow me."

Sean marched to Lisa's office.

Lisa was horrified to find that we were still at the studio and not on our way to the BBC Theatre. Then Sean dragged me out from behind him and made her look at the dress. She actually screamed.

"Oh, she can't wear that!" she said, shaking her head vigorously.

"Tallulah picked it for me," I said miserably. "Because she hates me."

Lisa shook her head.

"No, it's not you she hates, Ruby, it's me. She's done this because I asked her to find you a dress; because she knows it's my job to get you on TV looking good. She's done it to spite me."

"Why does she hate you?" Sean asked her.

"Because," Lisa said, "once, a long time ago, when we were both starting out, we were working on this film and there was this cameraman that we both liked the look of. Tallulah warned me to stay away from him, or else."

"And you didn't?" I asked, marvelling at Lisa's bravery.

"Well, you could say that – I married him," Lisa said, smiling at me. "She has never got over it. Come on, let's get this sorted."

The three of us went to see Tallulah, who was packing up for the day.

"She can't wear that," Lisa repeated, gesturing at the yellow confection without actually being able to bring herself to look at it. "It's awful!"

"I thought it suited her," Tallulah said pleasantly.

"It's awful," Lisa repeated.

"Well," Tallulah shrugged and glanced at the clock on the wall. "It's past six-thirty already. I haven't got anything else here for her to wear and nowhere else is open now." She smiled happily. "It's too late to change it."

"What about a costume?" Lisa said, her voice hardening slightly and tapping one of her long nails against her clipboard.

"Sure," Tallulah replied archly. "Which one of her ripped and dirty school uniforms do you want her to wear?"

"How about this?" Sean emerged from behind the costume rack. He was holding the lovely gold dress I had ripped.

"Perfect," Lisa said. "Get it on quick, Ruby, and I'll call and tell them you're on your way. Don't want them replacing you with a stand-by, do we?"

"It won't fit her," Tallulah said crossly. "She's too short for it and too wide."

"Then let it out and pin it up," Lisa said crossly. "I'm not asking you, Tallulah, I'm telling you. You have ten minutes." The two women looked each other in the eye for a moment until Tallulah finally realised she was beaten. She could bully a thirteen-year-old, but not the real Lisa Wells, who right at that moment looked just as scary and as formidable as the fake one.

"Fine," she told Lisa, even though it was clearly and obviously not.

Ten minutes later, having suffered minor blood loss through several vicious pin pricks, I walked out to the car in the gold dress. I might have been wider and shorter than Imogene, but after that yellow dress I felt fabulous in the gold gown, with its waterfall neckline and zig-zaggy hem. Tallulah even found me the gold shoes that went with it, which were ever so high and slightly too big, so that wearing them meant that I walked like a baby giraffe just finding its feet – but I didn't care because I wasn't a lemon any more.

"That's more like it," Sean said as he opened the car door for me.

"Lovely," my mum said with a little smile. "If a little bit old for you and I'm not too keen on those shoes."

Which, in my opinion, pretty much made it the perfect outfit.

There was no red carpet for this ceremony, which frankly I thought was a blessing. Afterwards there would be a photo call on the way to the after-show party, which Sean and I were allowed to walk into for publicity purposes but then had to leave with our parents immediately afterwards. I was glad really; it meant I wouldn't have to spend an evening trying not to look at Danny across a crowded room.

In the rush and tear up until this moment I hadn't had a chance to think about what it would be like to see him, let alone to perhaps even hand him the award for best newcomer. At the thought of it my stomach knotted and my mouth went dry.

I was still cross with him – really, really cross – but I missed him too. Before all of this happened he used to really make me laugh, make me feel happy and light. We could talk for hours about films and books and all the things we wanted to do with our careers. And sometimes we'd just hang out and say nothing, and it wouldn't matter because he was so easy to be with. And when he kissed me goodnight under the streetlamp outside my house? Well, it made me feel as if I were floating a little bit.

I hadn't really had a chance to miss him being my boyfriend yet, but I knew I would, and I knew it would be quite a long time before I stopped.

Sean and I left our parents who went to sit in the audience, and followed a highly stressed researcher called Carrie through a maze of corridors, where at last she showed us into the green room (which was actually orange) where the rest of the presenters waited.

It was like an A-Z of British soap actors, all of the most famous people in TV in one room together. But when Sean and I walked in for a second, for just one single breath, they all stopped talking and looked at him.

And that, I decided, was the difference between a real star, with his starriness built into his blood and bones, and all the rest of us plain old actors. Sean had a sort of magic all around him, which made you want to look at him and never stop.

"Sean," I said as he handed me a glass of orange juice.

"Yes, oh love of my life?" he replied, in a stupid soppy voice.

At that moment Carrie came in and called the first six presenters to go on set; the show had begun.

"Don't hate acting because of your dad," I told him,

as the first set of celebrity presenters filed out of the green room.

He took a quick step back from me, raising the palms of his hands.

"Whoa, I wasn't expecting that," he said, surprised. He ran his fingers through his spiky hair. "Look, I don't hate acting, Ruby. It's just that it's not fun any more. What I hate is all this: this endless life under a microscope where everybody thinks they know me, but nobody really does."

"I know you a bit, I think," I said. "And I know you hate being dragged around the world working non-stop and not having any kind of normal life. But, Sean, you can't let your dad make you hate acting. You were born to do it." Sean shrugged and looked at his feet.

"I really don't want to talk about this," he said uneasily.

"Look," I persisted, "I know everyone tells you this – but you are good, better than good – you're amazing! And you've got that special something that sets you apart from the crowd." I nodded at the few run-of-the-mill celebrities left in the room to make my point. "I don't want you to waste your talent, or use it up or lose it, because of what your dad is doing to you."

Sean took my hand and smiled into my eyes, and for

about five seconds I actually was in love with him.

"You really care about me, don't you, Ruby?" he asked me.

I nodded. Sean looked at me, his expression full of regret.

"I just can't see how things are ever going to change with Dad. Until I'm legally old enough to be free of him, I'll have to put up with it; right now I have nowhere else to go." We looked at each other intently. "I've met some great people here," he said sadly. "And I'm really going to miss you when I go. It would be great to stay friends with you, Ruby Parker."

I smiled up at Sean.

"But maybe we can." As I spoke Sean glanced over my shoulder and dropped my hand suddenly.

"Oh – hey, man," he said awkwardly.

I turned around and saw Danny staring at us.

"I spoke to Anne-Marie last night," he said coldly. "She told me I'd got everything wrong about you and him. I didn't believe her at first but she spent so long bending my ear I thought it had to be true. So, idiot that I am, I came backstage to find you and try and tell you how sorry I am." He looked from me to Sean, his face a mask of ice. "Looks like I've got nothing to apologise for."

"Hey, man...!" Sean began, but Danny had turned on his heel and gone.

"I'm sorry," Sean said. I sipped my juice without tasting it and shrugged.

"Don't be," I said, forcing myself to be brave. "It's not your fault."

Sean looked uncomfortable.

"Actually, Ruby..." Just at that moment Sean's mobile phone beeped and he took it out of his pocket.

"Mmm," he said thoughtfully. He glanced up at me. "Look, I have to do something, but when I come back I've got something to tell you and Danny, something that will put things right. Tell Carrie I'll be back in a few seconds."

"But the show's already started," I said anxiously. "Carrie will have an aneurism if you aren't here when she comes to get you. I will!"

"We're not on for ages," Sean told me with his easy smile. "We're the grand finale. I'll be back in time, I promise."

The minutes ticked by and one by one the celebrity presenters filed out of the green room to go on stage, until there was just a handful of us left. And Sean was not back.

"Hey," Carrie stopped short as she ran into the room. "Where's Sean?"

"Um… in the loo," I said unconvincingly.

"What?" Carrie looked worried. "Where is he really? You're on next, Ruby. I'll get killed if you don't both go on; it's Sean they want really." She bit her lip when she realised what she'd said and smiled at me apologetically.

"I'm sorry, but you know what I mean," she said. I nodded. I wasn't offended. It was after all the truth.

"I do," I said. "Don't worry, I'll find him."

I fished out my mobile that Mum insisted I took with me in case I went missing again and dialled Sean's number, planning to ask him where he was and to tell him to get back here now. But as I rang his number, I discovered I didn't have to. I knew exactly where Sean was because I could hear his phone ringing.

Holding my phone in front of me I followed the tone until I could hear it quite loudly.

There was a series of three doors in the corridor and the ring was coming from one of those.

The first one I tried was locked.

The second was empty.

In the third one I found Sean.

And Anne-Marie.

Kissing.

Each other.

"Oh, good! You found him." Carrie appeared right behind me and barged past me to get to Sean. She elbowed Anne-Marie out of the way and grabbed Sean by the arm with total disregard for his star status, and propelled him as fast she could towards the stage. "Come on, Ruby," she yelled over her shoulder. "We've got two minutes."

I watched Sean being dragged away by Carrie, glancing anxiously back over his shoulder as he went. I tuned round and looked at Anne-Marie.

"You said he didn't fancy you and you didn't fancy him," I said flatly. "Funny that, because snogging the face off each other usually indicates exactly the opposite."

"I know," Anne-Marie said, twisting her fingers. "But you see, we couldn't tell anyone."

"But..." I struggled to find the words. "Why? Why not? If you had told just me and Danny then—"

"Because Sean's father..." Anne-Marie started.

"RUBY PARKER GET HERE NOW!" Carrie hollered

down the corridor, with the ruthless determination that only a television researcher on a short-term contract can know.

I shook my head at Anne-Marie and started to walk as fast as I could in my high heels after Carrie and Sean.

"You could have told me," I said.

"Ruby, I'm sorry!" Anne-Marie called out after me. "Just let me explain!"

In a daze I caught up with Carrie, who rolled her eyes at me and shepherded Sean and me to the edge of the set. I felt the palm of her hand in the small of my back as we waited to go on.

"Ruby..." Sean said.

"Shhhhhh," Carrie hissed at us.

The show's presenter was announcing us.

"...and now for showbiz's most popular childhood sweethearts, Sean Rivers and Ruby Parker!"

"Go, go, go!" Carrie said in our ears and she gave us a little shove. I stumbled forward but Sean caught my hand and steadied me as we walked on to the stage to the sound of applause and cheers.

"I was going to fix it," Sean said in my ear as we smiled and waved at the audience still holding hands.

I yanked my hand out of his without breaking my smile, and waved it at the audience.

"You are nothing but a fake," I told him through my grimly grinning teeth. "Your whole life's fake."

"Do you think I don't know that?" Sean said under the noise of the audience as we walked over to the podium. "Do you think I don't hate it?"

"Do you hate it?" I asked him as we took our places. "Or is that just fake too?"

I looked at our lines which had been taped to the podium on the back of a card. We hadn't had a chance to rehearse them like all the other award presenters. All we knew was that we had to read one line each in turn as we announced the nominees, and then wait for clips from each of the four shows to be screened before finally opening the gold envelope and announcing the winner.

"Ladies and gentlemen," Sean and I began together. The audience laughed and so did Sean and I, grinning at each other like idiots. It should have been us winning the award for 'Best Fake Friendship on an Award Show'.

"Please accept our apologies," Sean said, turning his smile on the audience. "We only got this gig this afternoon because of poor Sindy Torrington's bad luck. And we'd like to take this opportunity to wish her a speedy recovery." Sean let loose his dazzling smile and the audience clapped again.

"I'll let the beautiful Ms Parker take the first line," he

said, giving me a little bow. I beamed at him and read the first line.

"Ladies and gentlemen, Sean and I are very glad to be here to present possibly the most important award of the evening, the award that announces the future of British soap…"

We read out the nominees' names without any more problems, and when they showed each one of them on the big screen I was relieved to see that Danny was in his seat. As they flashed his picture up on screen he was resting his chin in his hands, looking nervous. I could tell by looking at him that he really wanted to win the award.

As we watched the clips of each of the nominees in action being screened, Sean covered his radio mike with his hand. I did the same.

"Ruby, I didn't mean it to happen, with me and Anne-Marie," Sean whispered in my ear as we watched the big screen. "We only got together when she came up to the set. You had split up with Danny before that. You know it wasn't my idea to have a fake romance between us…"

"You *kissed* me," I hissed at him. "It was in the papers. You might have seen it in one of the five million copies that were knocking around?"

"I didn't know they were going to think that – I was just messing round," Sean insisted.

"Yeah, you were," I told him. "With my life. Messing around with my life. You could have at least told *me* about Anne-Marie."

"I know, but you don't know what would happen if Dad found out about Annie. You don't know what he would have done to me, and I'd never be able to see her again. I just wanted something for myself... I really like her, Ruby." Sean stopped talking as we both realised at once that the clips had finished and the audience were waiting for us to announce the winner.

"Young love," Sean said, as he uncovered his mike with an apologetic smile and a shrug. "You think the whole world will wait for you." The audience erupted into laughter.

Sean handed me the envelope. I took it and realised that my hand was trembling – from anger with Sean and Anne-Marie, and nerves for Danny, who I really, really wanted to win.

I slid my finger under the seal on the envelope and opened it.

"Please let it be Danny. Please let it be Danny," I repeated under my breath as I slid the card out of the envelope.

It was blank.

"Turn it over," whispered Sean.

I turned it over and read the name on the card.

I couldn't speak, and the moment of silence stretched out like years until at last Sean took the card from my hand and read the name out himself.

"And the award for best newcomer goes to Tatiana Khan for *The Dentists!*"

In that moment images of the three losers flashed up on the screen. When it showed Danny, all I could see was that he was leaving his seat.

Without thinking, I tottered on my heels out from behind the podium to the edge, where I could see Danny walking up the steps to the exit at the back of the seating.

Tatiana walked up to me and shook my hand, probably thinking I had come out to the edge of the stage to greet her. She kissed me on each cheek and was clearly waiting for me to escort her back to the podium. I looked at the double doors Danny had just left by and then back at the podium.

"You go on," I told Tatiana. "There's something I have to do."

I knew that my mum, Lisa Wells, Sylvia Lighthouse and anyone who had ever had any kind of career would be appalled at me running off the stage in the middle of the ceremony. I knew that as soon as I realised what I had done I would be appalled at *myself*. But I had to go.

I had to go after Danny because whatever happened

between us I knew how much he would be hurting now, and even if we were over I at least wanted him to know the truth.

That was when I fell off the stage.

I had been trying to get down the steps too quickly in the too-high heels, and the too-long hem of the dress got trapped under one of the heels, sending me tumbling forward and sprawling on my face.

"Ow!" I said, and for a moment I felt like sitting there on the floor of the theatre, with the eyes of the nation and the nation's celebrities glued to me, and bawling like next-door's toddler.

But I didn't. The show must go on, I decided. Even if it was one as miserable, embarrassing and as stupid as mine.

I got up, dusted myself down, did a little curtsey and went after Danny.

Just as I reached the exit I heard Sean say, "Excuse Ruby, she must have needed the bathroom."

"Well she did say it was an emergency," Tatiana added.

Everybody laughed.

Backstage, in the corridors of the BBC Theatre again, I could just see Danny's figure turning the corridor as I ran after him, stumbling and tripping with nearly every step, until I finally slid the shoes off my feet and went on, barefoot.

"Danny!" I shouted again. "Wait, I need to talk to you!"

The figure stopped and turned around and I almost ran right into him. Except it wasn't Danny. It was a very short security guard.

"Can I help you, miss?" the security guard asked.

"I... thought you were someone else," I said miserably. "Sorry."

The security guard shrugged and gave me a sympathetic smile.

"Do you want me to page anyone for you, Miss Parker?" he asked me.

"No thanks," I said, feeling deflated and defeated all at once. "I'll be fine."

I turned around and padded back along the cool smooth surface of the corridor towards the main auditorium.

Now that the heat of the moment had cooled, I

reflected on what I had done: walked off stage in the middle of a live television show; fallen flat on my face in front of millions; run screaming like a mad person after a short security guard; and to cap it all I realised, as I walked back down a totally empty corridor, I had lost my shoes. Tallulah's shoes. Who knew what revenge she'd take on me for that.

I sat down heavily on the bottom step of a staircase and looked at my toes.

In the distance I could hear the laughter and applause from the show as it came to an end. Soon this empty corridor would be full with celebrities and I would have to face Mum and Lisa and Sean and try to explain what I had done.

I had made a fool of myself on TV for nothing.

I didn't appear to have any friends left.

In a few days time my part in the filming of *The Lost Treasure of King Arthur* would be mainly over and I'd be back at Sylvia Lighthouse's Academy for the Performing Arts as officially the most unpopular girl in the school, possibly the country, if not the entire world.

I sighed.

A pair of black and white Puma trainers appeared in my line of vision as I stared at the floor. I knew those trainers.

Slowly I looked up.

It was Danny, holding the gold shoes.

"Do these belong to you?" he asked me. He didn't look angry, I thought. He looked sort of sad and tired.

I nodded.

"I was chasing you," I said, figuring I might as well tell him before he read it in the papers. "But they don't really fit me so I took them off." Danny knelt down on the floor and slid a shoe on to each foot in turn.

"Whomsoever these shoes don't really fit," he said, "I shall apologise to profusely." He sat back on his heels and looked at me.

"I'm sorry," he said. "I'm an idiot."

"Well..." I couldn't entirely contradict him. "You were a bit. You should have trusted me." I sighed. "But I suppose I've just found that you can't always trust your friends." Danny shook his head.

"You can," he said. "Anne-Marie was there when I walked off the show. She told me about her and Sean. She said there had never been anything going on with you two. She told me that last night, but for some reason I couldn't believe it. I don't know why."

"Because you'd made up your mind," I said. "You think I've been chasing Sean since the moment I met him. Since before I met him."

"You had his poster on your wall," Danny said.

I thought for a moment.

"Before I met him, when he was just a poster on my wall, well, yes, then I did have a bit of a crush on him," I said honestly. "But the minute I met him in real life, that crush had gone. I realised that he is just a boy. A brilliant, talented boy who I really like, but he's not you, Danny. I wanted to be with you and you wouldn't believe me."

"I suppose I didn't think I could compete with him," Danny said.

I laughed, which made him frown a little bit.

"Can I compete with the thousands of girls who write you love letters every week?" I asked him. Danny's answering smile was rueful.

"That's different," he said. "They're not you."

"And Sean's not you," I said.

Danny edged a little closer to me on his knees.

"I am an idiot," he said again. "A total thicko."

"Yes," I said, nodding, "you are. But then again I don't suppose my behaviour would win me the final of *Junior Mastermind* either."

"I nearly spoiled everything by getting too serious," Danny added.

"You did," I agreed. "You are an idiot and you are a

thicko, but that doesn't mean that I don't really care about you and that I don't sort of... well, actually – you know – love you, I suppose. Because... um, I do."

I swallowed hard. I had never said that kind of thing to anybody before in my life. And it hadn't been *quite* as poetic and romantic as I had imagined.

"Really?" Danny said, smiling broadly. "You do?"

"Well, yes," I said, feeling my cheeks burning. "But let's not go on about it, OK?"

Danny nodded. "Well just so you know," he said. "I do – that thing you said – as well."

"Well, good," I said, managing to smile back at him. "I'm sorry you didn't win the best newcomer award. You should have."

Danny shrugged. "Oh, that doesn't matter," he said. "All I want to know is will you be my girlfriend again, Ruby?" He picked up my hand.

I thought for a moment even though I knew the answer.

"I will," I said lightly. "But on one condition."

"What's that?" Danny said, taking my other hand and edging a little nearer still.

"That from now on, we trust each other, don't get too serious, and we remember we are not from Verona," I said.

"We will," Danny said, knowing exactly what I meant as he brought his lips a little closer to mine. "I promise that we will."

And he kissed me then, and I felt as if I were floating a little bit.

"Oh, thank goodness!" I heard Anne-Marie exclaim. "You've made it up." She blew a sharp puff of air out of her mouth so that a little bit of her long blonde hair wafted upwards.

"You again," I said coldly. "You keep turning up in the most unexpected places. How did you even get in here, anyway?"

"Oh, Daddy got me in. Look, Ruby, let me explain..." Anne-Marie began.

But just at that moment my mum and Jeremy Fort (who I didn't even know was there) came rushing towards me.

"Oh, Ruby, we've found you," Mum said in relief.

"I wasn't running away again..." I said.

"No, I know," Mum told me hurriedly. "Look – I had a call from Nydia's mum on my mobile. Nydia's collapsed. She's in hospital."

"Action!"

Chapter
Twenty-two

It really was winter at last. The days had suddenly got cold and the last leaves on the trees had fallen. I looked out the patio window in Nydia's house on to the garden where I stood and argued with Danny a few weeks earlier, and I watched the trees at the end of the garden, the stark black of their bare branches bristling against the flat pale sky.

None of the last few weeks seemed real any more. Getting the part in the film, driving out of school with Imogene Grant, acting with Jeremy Fort, meeting Sean Rivers, walking the red carpet. Even the award ceremony all seemed like a dream. I could not believe that any of it had ever really happened to me. But it had.

And some of it was wonderful and brilliant. And some of it was awful.

But the worst thing that had happened during those strange few weeks was that I nearly lost Nydia. I nearly lost my best friend, my almost twin, for good.

I *nearly* did.

"What are you thinking?" Nydia asked me from the sofa where she was resting.

"That life gets stranger every day you get older," I said, turning round to smile at her. "And that I should have been your friend instead of disappearing off to that film set. If I hadn't got that part then none of this would have happened."

Nydia shook her head.

"Nothing that much really did happen," she said. "I went on a stupid crash diet and fainted, cracked my head open, got some stitches and a good telling off. That's all that happened really."

"Nydia," I said, sitting down on the sofa next to her. "You'd stopped eating. If you'd carried on you could have been really sick. You could have died."

Nydia and I looked at each other for a moment.

"I know that now," Nydia said softly. "But I was so angry when I was doing it I didn't think about what would happen to me. I just wanted to be thin; I thought it would solve everything. And I blamed you because I was so angry inside that I just wanted someone to be angry at. It wasn't your fault, Ruby. I've had this secret feeling for a long time that I'm sort of stuck in the shadows, that nothing ever happens to me. I don't get the part in the film or the celebrity boyfriend. Or *any* boyfriend. I wanted someone, something to blame. I blamed you, and I blamed myself for being fat; I used it as an excuse. It was easier to deal with than the truth."

"What is the truth?" I asked her, hugging one of her mum's cushions on to my lap.

"That so far I just haven't been good enough," Nydia said.

"That's not true, you have…" I started, but she shook her head.

"I haven't, Ruby," she said. "And if anything, you've helped me see that, because I didn't really understand what I was doing until you brought Imogene to see me."

It had been Imogene's last day, she was flying back to California, but when I phoned her and told her what had happened to Nydia, she put back her flight and went to the hospital to sit with her.

Nydia couldn't believe it when I walked into her room with Imogene Grant.

"Hi, Nydia," Imogene said, in her soft, gentle voice. "Would you mind if I talked with you for a while?" Nydia shook her head as she struggled to sit up in bed.

"Do you mind, Ruby?" Imogene asked me, and I knew that she wanted me to leave. I shook my head and waited outside for an hour before Imogene came out again. I hadn't ever asked Nydia what she and Imogene talked about that afternoon because I felt it was just between them.

"Imogene told me," Nydia said, "that every actor, no matter how talented, just has to wait for their moment to come. That they spend their whole life waiting for that first moment and that sometimes it never comes. Or sometimes it only comes once and never happens again. She said if I wanted to be an actor I had to be strong enough to face that possibility."

"Your mum said you'd had lots of interest since your episodes of *Holby City* aired," I said.

"Yes," Nydia said. "But I don't want to play another fat sick girl. That was the other thing that Imogene made me see."

I waited for Nydia to continue, watching her as she picked at the hem of her jumper sleeve.

"She told me that by crash-dieting I was letting food rule me; I was making myself its slave and turning it from being some everyday thing into an obsession. She said if I let it go on it could have ruined my life, like it nearly did hers."

"Heavy," I said, not knowing exactly what else to say.

"I know," Nydia said. "She's so nice... well, you know. She talked to my mum and dad for ages and gave them the number of a nutritionist who can help us all eat more healthily. And now Mum knows how I feel, and knows how to help me, I feel so much better. I feel like I'm in *control* of my life now." Nydia shot me a rueful grin. "Well, you know, as much as anybody can be when they've got my mum as a mum."

I nodded sympathetically.

"I can't wait for you to be back at school," I said. "Anne-Marie will not shut up about Sean. It's Sean this and Sean that. Blah, blah, blah, blah!"

"And what about Sean?" Nydia asked me, giggling. I shrugged.

"To be fair," I said, "he will not shut up about Anne-Marie either."

If it hadn't been for one other discovery I'd made since finishing work on the film, then what happened with Sean and his dad might have been the most surprising thing of all.

On the last day of filming, just after Sean and I had wrapped our last scene and were walking back to our trailers, a black cab pulled into the lot. A woman with reddish brown hair, wearing a white trouser suit, got out and paid the driver.

She turned and looked around her.

"I don't believe it," Sean said, standing stock still.

"What?" I joked. "Don't tell me it's another fake girlfriend?"

It hadn't taken me long to forgive Sean and Anne-Marie, who had admitted they should have told me when they got together, even if Sean's dad would probably have bricked them both up in separate rooms if he ever found out. Besides, I couldn't stay cross with them: once I knew that Nydia was going to be OK, I was too happy about being back with Danny again to be cross at anyone.

"That," Sean said, staring at the woman who was now staring just as hard at him, "is my mother."

"Sean!" the woman called out and ran towards us.

"What do you think you're doing here?" Sean's dad bellowed from the open door of Sean's Winnebago. He must have seen her getting out of the taxi.

"I've come to get my son, if he wants to come with me," Catherine Rivers said, her chin high. She looked at Sean and her face softened. "Sean, there's so much to say, to explain, but you should know the only reason I haven't been in touch is because I thought you hated me," she said. "*He* told me you hated me. If I had known how much you needed me, Sean – you have to believe me."

I looked at Sean and I could see tears standing in his eyes.

"I don't understand..." he said, looking at his father.

"You don't have custody," Pat Rivers said, his face so red that it looked like it might explode. He marched over to us and stood opposite Sean's mum. "You have zero rights."

She glared at him, and I thought she was a little bit afraid, even if she was hiding it.

"All I need is my son to want to come with me and I think you'll find I get all the rights I need." She looked intently at Sean.

"Sean, I'm sorry I've let you down. But now I know for sure what you're going through I'll get you away from all of this, if you want me to. You can live somewhere where people won't harass or point at you. You can go back to school and make real friends, have a real life. And you won't have to act again unless you want to."

"Really?" Sean said in disbelief.

"No," Pat Rivers said. "You can't. You've made

contracts. It would cost me millions to break them."

"Lucky then," Sean's mum said without breaking eye contact with her son, "that *Sean's* got millions. It's up to your son. No court in the world will keep you from living where you want to, I promise you. And I know that you and I hardly know each other now, but I promise you I never stopped loving you or being so proud of you. I worried about you every day. I longed for you to get in touch with me. And then Imogene passed your message on to me."

"Message?" Sean asked her, totally bewildered.

"Why, you little..." Pat Rivers lunged at Sean but somehow, before I knew it, I was standing between him, his fists and his son. He stopped himself from hitting me with millimetres to spare.

"It was me," I told him, lifting my chin so I could look him in the eye. "I asked Imogene to tell his mother the truth. Sean had nothing to do with it."

"This is nothing to do with you," Pat Rivers growled at me. He took a step closer but before he could, Sean's mother put her arm across both Sean and I, guiding us back behind her.

"He said you didn't want me," Sean said, fighting to keep his voice steady as he pointed at his father. "He said you didn't want to know. Is that true?"

"Oh, my darling," Catherine Rivers said, with tears in her voice. "I've never stopped loving you, not for a second. I was weak and foolish. I should have kept on trying to reach you, but I gave up. You always looked so happy on TV. I'd do anything to make up the years I've lost with you."

"Mom!" Sean said and suddenly he was in his mum's arms and they were squeezing each other so tightly I didn't think they would ever let each other go.

"You can't do this!" Pat Rivers shrieked, just as Imogene, Jeremy, Art and two security guards ran across the lot towards us.

"You can't do this!" Sean's dad shrieked again as the security guards held him back.

"Mr Rivers," Art said, fronting up to Sean's dad even though he was a foot or so shorter than him. "It's quite clear that Sean wants some time with his mother. If you have any sense, I suggest you let him be and go and talk to your lawyers."

"I will!" Pat Rivers had shouted, turning on his heel and marching back towards the Winnebago. "And you *will* be hearing from my lawyers."

I looked at Jeremy and Imogene and we looked at Sean, sobbing in his mother's arms, and very, very quietly we walked away and left them on their own.

Which was why it was a bit of a shock a week later when we found out that Sean had enrolled at Sylvia Lighthouse's Academy for the Performing Arts and that he was going to live in London with his mother, at least until he finished school.

Anne-Marie hadn't shut up about it since. And as for Sean? Well, he told me *The Lost Treasure of King Arthur* was going to be his last film for a long time.

"But you're not giving up on acting?" I asked him. He grinned at me and ruffled my hair.

"How could I give up acting?" he said. "After all, I was born to do it."

The last and most surprising surprise had been when I got home from school one day and found Jeremy Fort sitting in my kitchen.

"Hello, Ruby," he said. I blinked at him but he didn't go away.

"Hello," I said uncertainly, just in case he was a hallucination.

"Your mum's upstairs. She invited me over for dinner." I nodded and sat down at the table. Everest hauled himself up on to the table top and looked menacingly at Jeremy. He didn't like strangers until they gave him food.

"It's nice to see you and everything, Jeremy," I said, lowering my voice, "but sometimes you're too polite for your own good. You don't have to come to dinner just because Mum asked you to. In fact, it might be better if you didn't. *She's got a bit of a crush on you.*"

Jeremy Fort laughed so loudly that Everest vacated the table.

"I know!" I said. "Funny, isn't it?"

"Ruby, why do think I'm here?" he said.

I shrugged. "Because you are very nice and have a problem saying no," I said.

"Not exactly," Jeremy said, leaning closer to me and whispering himself this time. "*It's because I've got a bit of a crush on your mum.*"

"Pardon?" I said.

"You heard," Jeremy said, winking at me.

"OK then," I said. "Well, that's... nice."

Just then Mum had come in from where she must have been hovering about in the hall.

"Oh, good, you're back," she said, as if nothing

amazing like my *mum* going out with an international film star and thespian had happened. "Risotto for tea anyone?" My cat meowed enthusiastically.

"Not you, Everest," we all said at once.

The door to Nydia's living room opened and Sean, Anne-Marie and Danny piled in, their arms full of DVDs.

"I think we rented the whole store," Sean said, dropping his bundle on to the rug.

"It was quite hard to find a film without Sean in, actually," Danny said, winking at me as he sat next to me.

"That's because he's so talented," Anne-Marie said fondly, looking at Sean as if she couldn't quite believe that he was really here.

"So exploited you mean," Sean said wryly.

"Thanks, guys," Nydia said. "It's really great for you all to come round here and hang out with me. I'm sure you could be doing something more exciting."

"Do you know what?" Sean said, sitting down on the rug and smiling at Nydia. "For me there is nothing better than spending a whole afternoon doing nothing but just hanging out with friends. Real friends."

"Yes, it is good, isn't it?" Anne-Marie said. "Hey, I know, we should plan something different for every day during the holidays: ice skating, shopping, cinema, shopping, galleries, shopping…"

"Actually," I said a bit nervously, "I can't make any plans for the holidays."

Everyone looked at me curiously, except for Danny who already knew what I was about to tell them.

"Why not?" Nydia asked me.

"Well, you know how Mum and Jeremy Fort are an item now," I said, still with a little air of disbelief. They all nodded. "He's in Los Angeles at the moment, starting work on a new movie." I allowed myself a little smile.

"He wants me and Mum to spend the holidays out there with him. Dad doesn't mind as long as he gets me for the next holidays so – we're going!"

"Christmas in Hollywood?" Nydia whistled through her teeth. "Cool!"

"Not *that* cool," Sean said wryly.

"Oh, shut up," Anne-Marie said mildly. "Cool as far as *we* are concerned. Imagine all the stars you'll see!"

"I know," I said. "And, well, Adele's got a few people for me to meet out there."

"What? Do you mean auditions?" Nydia exclaimed.

"No, just meetings, networking, that sort of thing," I

said. "It won't come to anything. I'll be back before you know it."

My four friends looked at me and at each other.

"Totally brilliant!" Anne-Marie said.

"Amazing!" Nydia said. "Just imagine!"

"I know," Danny said, smiling at me and holding my hand. "Get ready USA. Ruby Parker goes to Hollywood!"

g teen Magazine's girl! kraZee question time

Every week you write, e-mail or text in your questions to put to a different star. This week we're putting your best and funniest questions to budding film star Ruby Parker!

1. From Lucy Mills, Essex:
Ruby, I loved you in *Kensington Heights*! Are you ever coming back?
Ruby: I don't have any plans to at the moment, but I might do one day!

2. From Sasha Danes, South Wales:
What's snogging Sean Rivers like?!
Ruby: I have never snogged Sean so I wouldn't know, thank you very much!!

3. From Lizzy Smith, South London:

Are you nervous about when the film you have just made comes out in the summer? What if everybody hates it?

Ruby: I am a bit nervous, of course, but if you want to be an actor you have to be able to take criticism. I really loved making it and I think that if you like a fun, fast-paced action adventure then you'll love *The Lost Treasure of King Arthur*. Go and see it as soon as it comes out!

4. From Lily Fehim, Herts:

Do you have any diamonds of your own now – or will you have to steal some more?

Ruby: Oh that was so embarrassing! I certainly won't "steal" any more and no, I haven't got any of my own – I'm still saving!

5. From Phoebe Day, Suffolk:

You've been in a soap, made a film. What are you planning to do next?

Ruby: Well, I haven't got any firm plans, but in a few days I'm flying to Los Angeles to visit Jeremy Fort on the set of his new film. I am really looking forward to going to America. I don't know what will happen when I get there but I just know that going to Hollywood is going to be really exciting!

Next week put your crazy questions to award-winning actress Tatiana Khan!

It wasn't Jeremy Fort's Rolls Royce picking Mum and me up from the airport that blew me away.

It wasn't even his massive mansion with two swimming pools, a tennis court and a stable full of horses that really did it.

It was later that night, when I went out on to the balcony and looked up at the hill and saw those famous white letters.

That was when I realised I was really here, in this magical place built of thousands of hopes and dreams, and where some, just some of those dreams come true.

I'm in Hollywood now.

Coming soon...

Ruby
Parker

Hollywood
Star

ROWAN COLEMAN